Guruianu mesmerizes with the slow burn of his evocative prose in these compelling stories. He probes the mysteries of 'small things set in motion' with stunning precision and a remarkable degree of tenderness. *Body of Work* is a brilliant collection that explores humanity in all its facets of darkness and light. Superb!
— Meg Tuite, author of *Bound By Blue*

ISBN-13: 978-1-937677-50-3
Library of Congress Control Number: 2013941560

Fomite
58 Peru Street
Burlington, VT 05401
www.fomitepress.com

Body of Work
Stories

Andrei Guruianu

Fomite
Burlington, VT

Acknowledgments

Grateful acknowledgment is made to the editors of the following magazines where versions of these stories first appeared:

Connotation Press: "Beginnings"

The Summerset Review: "Body of Work"

Word Riot: "Friendly Advice"

Dogmatika: "After the Party"

Red Clay Review: "Hawking"

Egophobia: "The Man of Many Names"

I am also extremely grateful to the Corporation of Yaddo for providing me with the space, time, and inspiration for several of these stories to come to light.

Contents

Body of Work

It was not the first time he'd looked at his hands and fidgeted nervously with the tips of his fingers, rubbing them against each other, burying them in the smooth skin of his palms. Sometimes he rubbed them in a deliberate cleansing motion, then pocketed the closed fists inside his jacket to resist the urge to look again.

Today, the old man was once again keenly aware of his hands. He rubbed his fingertips more than usual. At the newspaper office the clerk behind the counter gave him a look that made him think she noticed. Years ago his wife had noticed them. His ex-wife now. She'd pointed them out quite often. His hands were soft, pale, and showed no lines, not unlike his blushing cheeks that even in his later years retained a youthful color. Today, the weather outside had made them worse, the cold air calling to the surface rude splotches of red.

He had delicate hands, as his wife put it tactfully, but he knew what she meant.

"Is this it, sir?" The clerk had to ask twice, for the old man was lost in his thoughts.

"Yes. That's all. How much to run it for one week?" He fumbled with his checkbook, knowing he'd have to place the paper and pen, and therefore his hands, upon the counter.

He'd often avoided bringing attention to his hands when he was around his wife. It had been easier that way. He could sense how she held back and relented with indifference when he tried to hold her. And when she left him finally, he wondered if it was more than his inability to give her a child, to make her happy. He resented that she'd moved on as easily as changing into a new outfit, and that in turn he'd become bitter, ashamed of himself. As he left the newspaper office he turned the wording of the advertisement over in his mind. "Female nude model wanted. Generous compensation. Call …"

Why had the woman asked, "Is this it, sir?" Should he have written more? And what else could he have written, after all? It was what he needed now that he finally had the time, but most of all the courage and the strength to get back to his work. After his wife left him he'd simply stopped. But as much as he wanted so earnestly to be caught up in his painting, he was despairingly unproductive. He sat for hours and hours in his garret on the second floor of his turn-of-the-century brownstone. He watched students walk back and forth on the sidewalk underneath his window. He watched shoppers with their fat bags, the cars in traffic inching to the light then lurching forward once again. He watched nothing. This is why he'd decided on the ad, something he'd never done, not even when his work was sought after and he needn't have paid if he'd merely made his intentions known. Women wanted to be painted by him.

His wife had been one of his first models, and his early shows were indeed tributes to her. The paintings were large, life-size reproductions of the old man's then ideal vision. In his eyes she was perfect, and he worked hard to capture her every detail until the woman on the canvas looked at any moment as if she would breathe. But that was a long time ago, and his work had gotten smaller since, a bit more abstract.

It had been more than ten years since his last solo exhibit was remanded to the back room of the gallery for permanent storage. The only other places he imagined one could find his work were stuffy attics or damp basements where the moisture slowly bit into the canvas, followed shortly by decay. Who would come to him if he didn't place the ad? He'd grown so isolated in the wake of his divorce that his name was a faint memory even among his colleagues. He'd become a stranger, alone, and only now, maybe now, because he knew what he had to look for, could he permit himself to think that it was time.

The old man let his thoughts become muddled as he

urged his aging frame against the January wind, making his way between the drab façades of recently erected towers, bright awnings and twisted window mannequins that stared out onto the street with eerie human likeness. He headed to his apartment on the edge of town, at least a twenty-minute walk to the university quarter, the neighborhood he'd lived in since retiring from his teaching post.

And although he'd been down many of these same streets before, he saw them now painted in a new light, with the vigor of a man roused from a stupor, a prolonged lazy sleep. He saw their cracks and crevices, their random drunken sidewalk patterns that marred the regular arrangement of the concrete slabs, the sudden and relieving break from the monotony of expectations.

When he reached the landing of his apartment building he unlocked the front door and pushed his weight against the solid slab of wood that sometimes expanded and stuck on humid days. A pall had settled on the city for a couple of weeks, and only recently had the wind begun to drive away the clouds, making room for the scent of pure, cold air.

Inside the door, the brownstone was clean, almost clinical. On the first floor was an apartment whose residents were often students in transition to more respectable housing. He seldom shared more than a nod with the occupants below him in the rare instances they met on the stairs or inside the common hallway before he climbed to the second floor.

As he walked up the stairs he realized he was happy to

get back to his rooms today. He was aware of a mild excitement that set in as he left the newspaper office.

It wasn't long until he received a call about the simple ad.

"Hello? Hi. I'm calling about the ad in the paper?" The voice on the other end sounded breezy, but practiced. He couldn't determine an age that fit the tone. The woman sounded interested, but distant. There was a short exchange.

"I can pay $100 an hour," he said.

She agreed, said something about "expecting," but he barely heard the end of her sentence. Something in the woman's voice made him nervous and agitated. His chest felt warm. Was she implying…? She was the first to call, and he was eager to start. "Is Saturday at six O.K.?"

"That's fine. That works just great for me."

"The address: 32 Hyacinth Lane."

Something bothered him. Something about the way the woman on the line had said goodbye. He waited for Saturday to come. In the meantime he made the necessary preparations and got all of his supplies ready.

At exactly six o'clock he heard the doorbell ring with a short burst. He pressed the buzzer. A curt knock followed shortly after and he opened the door to a woman with a confident smile who presented herself using a first and middle name that he imagined to be hyphenated. She offered her hand by way of introduction. He glanced down and then away, leaving the woman's hand to wilt. He clasped his own hands behind his back and stepped aside to allow her in, then closed the door and moved about the apartment. The hands remained hidden behind his back.

The old man thought that something about her was attractive, but not necessarily beautiful. At least not in the conventional sense of the word. Her face, neck and upper shoulders were mottled with freckles that looked as if they had been carelessly applied. Her nose was interrupted by a rude bump right below eye level. A few loose strands fondled her neck as she moved.

"There is an envelope with the money on the side table by the door."

It was awful to start that way. He was aware of the cold tone of his voice, the way he measured every word. But he had no choice. He was new at this. He wanted to sound professional, dignified. He didn't want to give off the wrong impression.

"Can I use your bathroom to change?" asked the woman, who'd been waiting in the same spot just inside the door.

"Yes, of course. I'm sorry. It's just around that corner, on the left. Don't mind the... I didn't think you'd need to..." He didn't finish the sentence. Behind his back he rubbed his fingertips.

The woman walked into the bathroom, leaving the old man to fidget in his place, trying to convince himself there was no need to be embarrassed. Maybe she wouldn't notice the mirror above the sink, the drops of soap that made his reflection quiver under the bare bulb that was missing its original enclosure. And maybe, he hoped, she wouldn't see the reddish stubble in the sink, the remnants of a patchy beard that grew on his boyish face. The face, along with his hands, had led his wife to remark more than once that he hardly looked touched. It was not meant as a compliment.

When the woman came out of the bathroom she had removed her clothes and was carrying them in her arms. The old man had placed a chair in the middle of the living room and invited her to sit, gesturing with his head toward the couch to deposit her clothes. Across from the chair, within a few feet, he'd set up his station. It consisted of an upholstered, gently slope-backed chair and a four-panel wooden screen. When he sat down, only his shoulders and head were visible from the other side.

There he sat behind his parapet, asked the woman to make herself comfortable, and told her that she didn't need to worry about keeping perfectly still. From the position she'd taken, slightly turned but still partially facing her employer, she could tell by the movement of the old man's shoulders and the frequent glance in her direction, that his hands were furiously working away at something. After several minutes he leaned forward out of his chair and stood up, coming out from behind the screen. He fastened his hands behind his back and approached her where she sat. He circled her, scrutinizing his subject as one would an artifact on the auction block.

Completing his circuit once around the chair, he noticed a brown blemish just below her collarbone, a raised birthmark most likely, that disturbed the otherwise smooth skin. His eyes also found on her upper arm a small but violent scar. It looked like a vaccination mark that had spilled beyond its proportions and drew dark skin into itself like two puckered lips. He walked back to his chair where he bent back upon his work.

At seven o'clock, the end of the hour, he announced that the session was over. After the woman dressed he asked with a little trepidation if she would come back at the same time next week. She agreed. He was relieved when she took the envelope and walked out the door and down the stairs without prolonging the awkward moment.

From his window he watched her disappear around the corner and he was once again left alone in his garret to observe the slow unraveling of spring. But he didn't mind that anymore. He looked forward to finishing what he'd begun.

And then the day came, unfolding with minute variations of the previous encounter. The woman wore roughly the same outfit, the envelope waited on the side table next to the door, and the middle of the room was arranged with the same chair and screen.

As soon as they had taken their respective places and the woman consciously assumed a different pose than before, she noticed that he did not dip his head as often and the fire that accompanied his earlier movements barely flickered. Something in his eyes, she thought, showed he was not happy. She began to think that it was her, and though she'd done this many times before, she began to be uncomfortably aware of his eyes upon her. She drew her arms that much tighter in a self-embrace.

The old man stood up from his chair as he'd done before and walked in meditation in his circle. When he came to the spot where his face lit up the last time, he simply stood, impassive. After what seemed like an eternity he gathered up the courage to say what he wanted to say.

"Could you please sit as you did last Saturday?"

The woman shifted in her chair, relieved that with a mere turn the old man looked happy again. He'd seen that mark, the birthmark just below her collarbone, and with a pivot went to work behind his screen.

The woman returned for a few more sessions and after the old man had searched and squinted as hard as he could he found nothing more. He'd exhausted his subject. When he didn't ask her to return again he couldn't tell whether she looked upset or relieved. If she was happy to go he didn't blame her. He knew that he could never stand as she did to feel someone else's eyes peel her open, make her painfully conscious of her own body.

When the woman left for the last time he did not watch her down the sidewalk. He went instead into the bathroom, splashed some water on his face and felt the softness of his cheeks that never betrayed what was missing inside. That's why his ex-wife had left. She'd wanted children. She wanted his children, the one thing he could never give her, so she made him feel like less than a man. The old man stood in front of the mirror, gripped the sides of the sink with his wet hands and looked up into the white bulb above.

"This is not my fault. You can't blame me for this."

And he knew as soon as he'd uttered those words that he'd go back to the newspaper office the following Monday morning and ask the woman behind the counter to run the ad one more time. He would walk down the same streets looking up into the same windows with their meticulous arrangement of limbs and clothes, no wind to disturb them, no wrinkles in the straight, unruffled lines. Nothing on the surface of those China doll white bodies. How he hated their blank eyes, the way they seemed to know while smugly saying nothing, betraying nothing of their thoughts. He'd bend his head toward the sidewalk and the beaten, bruised cement would comfort him.

He placed the ad for one more week. He waited. He was used to that, to the long years when he anticipated that something, anything would light the spark that disappeared when his wife grabbed her things and went out the door insisting, "Really, it's not you. You're a wonderful man. It's just…" and with that she was gone. What followed were months that blended into seasons, and in his mind the words played over and over again, "It's just…" "It's just…" – until he'd finally looked long enough at the pictures stacked together in boxes, the ones taken by the shore in the fifties when he still had a full head of hair and she still wore her bathing suit, the one as tight and intimate as a glove. Everything looked perfect, perfectly still, and from those pictures you could tell nothing more than that. It was then the reason became clear, how deceiving all of it was. It stared out at him, from some place sealed shut with forgetting and forgiveness, a monstrous, unspeakable thing, and now he saw it everywhere he turned, in everything that breathed and in all that didn't.

The phone rang mid-week. When he'd neglected to answer their calls, his friends had long given up on trying to coax him to come out. No one called these days unless it was necessary to do so. Unless it was business. The woman sounded younger than the first, and her voice less confident than he'd expected. They came to an arrangement as to the date and time, and when she hung up the old man sensed her words had a pleading tone, a need for reassurance that was hardly satisfied by goodbye.

She arrived a bit early the day of the session, dressed in a light top – it had gotten warmer outside – and a pair of jeans that flattered her frame. She brought with her the sweet scent of lilacs in bloom, still clinging to her skin and the folds of her clothes. He could have seen her in the past walking back and forth along the sidewalk. She was predictably beautiful.

A short exchange, then, "The bathroom is around the corner if you need to…"

She followed his instructions, taking with her a bag that had been resting on her shoulder since she'd come in the door. She came out shortly after with a green towel wrapped about her body, leaving bare only legs and shoulders.

"I've sat for an art class once at the university," she offered. "They only pay twenty dollars, so when I read your ad I was hoping no one else had called."

"No one else has called," the old man replied.

"Oh. Well, good for me then." She smiled.

"Make yourself comfortable." He gestured to the chair in the middle of the room and turned to take his own spot behind the screen.

She removed her towel, folded it next to the chair and sat down with legs crossed and one arm craned behind her back. He knew she was doing it because she thought he'd appreciate the artsy pose, just as he knew from the squint of her eyes that she believed he was an odd, eccentric, maybe perverted old man.

From his enclosure he stared intensely, his eyes flicking across her body in a desperate search. Minutes went by. He didn't move an inch. He could tell the girl was getting nervous because her cheeks became flushed. It wasn't the lack of clothes, not that. He knew it was his eyes that were making her feel inadequate.

Finally the old man stood and tried to find an answer in his routine, rounding the chair in contemplation. He went around once, twice, then back toward the screen, stopping short of the other side. He turned to the girl and said, "I'm sorry. This simply isn't working. You can still have the full amount."

The girl sat there and stared at the old man, still in the same twisted position she'd assumed at the start of the session. It had been less than half an hour. I know you don't understand, the old man wanted to say, but this won't do at all.

"I'm sorry. Did I do something wrong? If you need me to move I can. I mean, I've done this only once before and they didn't ask, but…" The old man cut her off, trying hard to check his annoyance.

"No. Nothing is wrong. It's not you, it's just… Look, please. The money is there."

The girl took up her towel and walked into the bathroom. She came out in her top and jeans with bag across one shoulder and picked up the envelope by the door. For a moment the old man was back on the shore, sand under his feet, arm around a firm, smooth waist. She reminded him so much of his ex-wife, the wonderful stillness preserved in those photographs that looked as if nothing could ever go wrong.

"Thank you for coming," said the old man halfheartedly. He was disappointed. When she was gone he watched her move down the sidewalk, and from a distance she looked no different than the dozens of other girls cluttering the arrival of dusk. But he knew otherwise.

Later that night in front of his mirror the old man looked again at his reflection, then up through the imaginary, endless extension of the ceiling. He sighed a deep, heavy sigh and murmured, "You can't blame me for this. You left me with no choice. You left me with nothing." Then he sunk his head into his chest and turned away from the glass.

That evening he decided to cancel the ad. The following morning he walked his usual route to the newspaper office, and as he approached the university he saw the man who stood outside its walls and played his two-string every spring and summer. He sounded as terrible as ever, and the old man thought that the musician knew he sounded terrible. But that didn't stop him. Every day, weather permitting, the man opened his black case with a few wrinkled bills and some coins tossed on the bottom. The old man didn't know exactly what tempted him to reach into his pocket that day – the awful music or his awareness that when the man's blunt, knobbed hands drew the bow, he was reminded of his own failings. The man didn't hide his weakness, his inadequacy. He had perfected mediocrity and all that he got in return were coins and pity.

Those thoughts passed in and through his mind and drifted away when the music faded in the distance. Back in the apartment, the days resumed a monotonous hum until one day the shrill sound of the phone interrupted the silence that had settled like a blanket through the rooms. He recognized the voice. It was the girl whose sitting he had ended.

"Hello," she said, apologized again, and could she not come back and sit for him once more, not for the money really, you understand, although that wouldn't hurt she said, but maybe this time it would turn out better. She'd read some things on proper posture.

The old man hated that she'd contacted him again. He did not like to be bothered; he liked to do things on his own terms. But he was tempted to try again. It was only when he saw these women, the ones he would have passed on years ago as lacking, that he'd been able to resume painting. He just needed the right one.

After a pause he agreed, and the day and time were arranged. When she arrived this time the old man was eager to get to work and didn't wait for her to come out of the bathroom before taking his usual place. She found him sitting half-hidden behind the screen, gesturing for her to sit. As she'd entered the apartment nothing about her struck him as terribly new. Same standard top, same flawless skin and hair that shone a healthy russet. Not a single disturbance.

He made a few agitated movements with the brush, desperately trying to make something of it. He asked her to shift, please, fold and unfold her arms, sweep her hair to the side. He walked around, his steps erratic. He clenched and unclenched his hands. The girl was visibly uncomfortable, but said nothing. She was probably questioning herself, the old man thought. Wasn't she beautiful enough? Wasn't she perfect for what he needed? Why couldn't he do something, anything, with what he saw? But the girl would never ask that.

"Is something wrong?" she said instead.

"I can't do this," the old man almost whispered.

"What is it this time?" The girl's poise shook slightly.

"Nothing. There's nothing." He took a breath. "Don't you understand? There is absolutely nothing wrong. You come in here and think that just because everyone else… and you expect me to… there's not one single scar, anywhere." That last part was not supposed to come out.

The girl looked down at her lap, then up again. She did not make a sound. The old man seemed to pour himself out to her, to accuse and ask for understanding at the same time. He turned and walked into the bathroom, ashamed at his tirade, his lack of control, realized his hands were two fists inside his pockets. But there wasn't anything more he could do. He was tired of searching in vain for what clearly wasn't there. He hoped she'd be gone by the time he came back out.

When he finally returned he noticed that the girl, encouraged by his absence, had wrapped the towel around her body and walked over to the old man's abandoned work. He watched as she stood there, possibly trying to see herself in the lines, but he knew she wouldn't recognize anything familiar. There was an outline that suggested form, but nothing more. She moved to a stack of paintings leaning along a wall beneath the window, the same one where he spent his hours, watching people passing back and forth. Where he did not need to hide his fingertips that rubbed against the damp, pink creases of his palm. The girl flipped through the paintings like old records, frantically looking for something.

"What are you doing?" he snapped.

"These are not portraits. They're not even pictures … of women. What are these?" the girl asked, her voice trembling with curiosity.

Every canvas showed a prominent dark spot or scar, or any other kind of aberration that glared like an angry eye and took up most of painting. In the background, the women that should have belonged to those marks were mere shade and shadow.

From the look on her face, he suspected that she understood all too well. But he wasn't sure if she was angry, upset, if anything at all. The girl dressed quickly and left the envelope on the table. At the click of the lock, the old man began to put his work away, vowed to himself to never pick it up again.

Subsequently, his days were spent in a cycle typical of his old age, a morning to night routine interrupted only by necessity. He let the mirror get dirty again, its surface cloudy with soap residue. It made his face and hands a bit more bearable as he shaved.

Several days had passed and the memory of the last girl was beginning to give him peace. He couldn't pick her out from the crowd outside his windows. It shocked him then when she rang the doorbell, insisted to see him. She said he wouldn't be disappointed, and he felt compelled to let her in.

As he opened the door she stepped through the opening. He watched as she put down her bag and dropped the shoulders of her summer dress, letting the light material crease about her ankles. When she turned her back slightly toward him, he noticed just below the shoulder line a small red mark. It curved like a closed eyelid. It was a perfect scar that still showed where her fingernail broke through the skin to pull back a small tear in the flesh. One drop of blood had dried and crusted over in a trail down to her lower back.

The old man realized that when the girl looked back over her shoulder and smiled she was waiting for his approval. "Paint me," he thought he heard her say, although he might have imagined it. But it was enough.

At the sight the old man took a step back. A thought went through his mind and it made him shudder. He gripped his hands until the knuckles looked like bone.

Hawking

In the distance the road looked like one long illusion. The highway with its stains of gasoline and motor oil burning under a midday sun shimmered and shook and disappeared as soon as we got close enough to watch them slide beneath the front of the old pick-up. One minute they were there, beautiful as rainbow smudges, welcome distractions of color, then nothing but what seemed like endless gray broken only by a solid blue ahead.

"Here. Here looks right," Joanie said.

I guided the tires over the rumble strips and pulled over onto the gravel that faded into a sunburnt field. We stepped down from the truck and stood a few feet from the road, our shoes crunching the dry grass. I knew why we'd stopped, though I hadn't seen him yet.

Without looking back at me, Joanie pointed her arm just above shoulder level. Out of the sky I saw it cut through the blue like the slow, elegant sweep of a blade. It glided toward the ground until two legs appeared from its belly and the beating of its wings threw up a small cloud of dust.

"Do you think it's him?" Joanie turned to look at me as she asked.

"It could be," I said. "I wouldn't doubt it if it was."

I asked Joanie if she wanted to stay a while, look a little longer.

"No. It's alright," she said, and we got back in the truck.

At the sound of the engine the hawk took off, a handful of dirt thrown into the wind.

I'd come to live with Carl and Joanie about a year ago. I was a floater, moving from family to family. I'd stay until they couldn't put up with me anymore and then I'd be passed on.

It went like that for years until Carl and Joanie took me in. Even with them I still got sent home from school. I was on probation for various infractions. But when they got a call from school or the police station to come pick me up, they didn't flip like the others and call Social Services. I couldn't blame people for that. I wouldn't want to deal with me either.

But Carl had this way about him. He didn't say anything so there was no chance for me to come back with a smart ass comment like, "You're not my father. I don't have to listen to you." He knew he wasn't my father. So when he would come and get me we'd get in his pickup truck and we'd drive out along the highway for miles until we came into the open where there were maybe a few scraggly trees shaking their branches in the air. He would pull up along the edge of the road and we would get out and walk into a cornfield that looked like it carried a permanent, yellow five o' clock shadow.

Carl wouldn't say anything until we'd walked some distance, and then all of a sudden he would lift his outback hat, as I liked to call it, wipe the sweat from his brow and replace it on his head with a "Here we are" as if he was merely letting out a breath.

The "here" often changed to a different highway, but I came to expect the trip, even looked forward to it after a while. We would be out there in those fields, alone with the grass and wind and clouds that dragged their shadows along behind them on the ground. Carl would be all quiet, and I would wonder if he would just leave me there in the middle of nowhere and drive off. I probably deserved it, but he never did.

Instead he would scan the horizon from behind a pair of dark shades that seemed permanently attached to his face. He was a welder by trade. You could tell by the scars on his forearms where the hot solder had bitten into the skin. Minutes would go by with Carl looking to the sky, saying nothing until I would lose my patience and blurt out, "What the hell are we doing here, Carl?" He would say, "Shhh," calm and composed, then point to somewhere above the flat line of earth and sky and I would spot a bird all alone out there with all that blue and white.

"Big deal," I said the first time we drove out together. He'd just picked me up out of a holding cell. I didn't give a damn about a dumb bird. Carl just said, "Shhh. Watch." And the bird hung up there like a kite, then swooped down, growing bigger as it came closer to the ground. Long, outstretched brown wings. "It's a red-shouldered," Carl said, and left it at that. The bird kicked up some dust as it touched down then took off again with something in its claws. It made no sound.

"That was a red-shouldered hawk. There's a lot of them here in the East, California, too," Carl explained on that first day. "Few more weeks and I'll have my hawking permit."

"You need a permit to watch birds?" I asked.

"No, not to watch."

"What for then?"

"With a permit you can catch those birds and train them," he explained.

From the look on my face Carl could tell I didn't understand why anyone would want to do something like that.

"Because they are as beautiful as they are wild. They have a mind of their own. They're not like others," Carl said.

On subsequent trips out along the highway, and there were plenty given my track record, Carl talked only about hawks. He never brought up the reasons why he had to take off from work to get me out of whatever bind I'd gotten myself in. He explained how the hawks could be trained in time to listen to commands, do tricks, return to you when you called. But they would always remain wild, that was always his word of caution.

"You never know when they will turn on you. You don't know when they will never come back," he warned. "They have a strong will."

Carl and Joanie were the last people I would stay with before I turned eighteen and graduated high school. On my birthday Joanie made dinner as usual and baked a cake with the numbers 1 and 8 on top. We ate dinner and I blew out the candles, then we had cake. After that day I was free to go wherever I wanted. Neither of them asked.

The next morning I woke up and went down to the kitchen where Carl and Joanie were already sitting around the table. Joanie was eating toast with homemade jam and Carl was slicing a piece of cheddar with the pocket knife he kept attached to his belt around the clock. Along with his sunglasses, it was another accessory that came to define Carl for me over the months we spent together.

I poured coffee and settled in a chair. "Morning," they said, and I said "Morning" right back.

"Carl was going to rip up the carpet in the basement today," Joanie said. "It's about had its due."

Carl knifed some more cheese, put it in his mouth with the blade of his knife then wiped it clean in the crook of his elbow. I couldn't tell if he was looking at me from behind his shades.

We sat like that until we finished breakfast, then Carl got up and walked down to the basement. I followed him and we began tearing the moldy carpet into pieces. That's how I ended up staying with Carl and Joanie.

Not long after that Carl got me a job at the same plant where he worked. I got used to the smell of my own hair burning as a spark flew onto my arms. Sometimes, when the day was done, Carl and I would go out along the same fields that had grown familiar to me, and we would try to get a hawk. Carl had gotten his permit and he was training hawks. He already had one at home. He wanted to get one for Joanie. Everything they did they had to do two ways.

It was Joanie who explained why there was this quiet, unspoken understanding between them, why they seemed inseparable even when hours would go by with nothing said between them. It was because neither of them had to give up anything in the relationship. Not even a name. By some twist of fate they shared the same last name. And even though they weren't related they had to go through some hell to prove it before the state. There was a different law than that of man that had brought them together and

Carl said he'd be damned if he would let some judge get in the way. They would be together, one way or another, Carl had promised her on a ride home once, tipping his neck to the back seat where he kept a shotgun. He spoke in suggestions.

Nothing changed now that we were out looking for hawks together other than the fact that I wasn't getting into trouble anymore. I knew where to scan for the birds' lazy glide right along the treetops, rarely higher, and would even pick them out before Carl had a chance to do so. I think it made him happy in some way.

Carl died right before I tuned 20. He died in his sleep, having shown no signs that it was coming. But who knows what kind of pain he was hiding behind those glasses, inside all that silence? Even if something was bothering him he wouldn't have said anything. Not even to Joanie. Not to bother her.

We buried Carl without an autopsy. He wouldn't have wanted one, Joanie said. At the cemetery there was me and Joanie, and Carl lying in a simple pine box. We laid his hat on his chest and I placed his blade at his feet. A few people from the plant came to pay their respects and the pastor said a few words. I threw some dirt that fell with a thud upon the wood.

Joanie went through the motions for a few days. At

times it seemed like nothing was different, nothing was wrong. The house was quiet the same way it was when Carl had been around. But you could tell she wasn't the same. It was as if she was lost within those rooms she knew by heart.

One day I came home from work and found her out by the shed that Carl had built for the hawks. The doors to the cages were open and looked like they'd been that way for some time. There was no point in asking the obvious.

"Do you think they'll make it?" I asked.

"I don't know. Maybe. I don't know. They kept together for a while, but then I lost them when they dipped behind the trees. I hope they will. They were good birds. They always came back when he called."

I knew Joanic wouldn't call after them. It would probably be better that way. And they would be all right, I thought, they were strong-willed birds.

Some weeks went by. I didn't know whether I should move out or not. I didn't know what would be more appropriate. I hadn't had to deal with that decision before. Joanie wasn't my mother, but it felt like I would be abandoning her nonetheless. If I stayed, I felt like I would be intruding on her ability to grieve. But she said nothing, and I said nothing. That's how Carl and Joanie did things, allowed them to sort themselves out.

One day Joanie said, "Let's go for a ride," and she got ready and went out to wait in the pick-up truck. She took the passenger seat before I caught up.

"Where do you want to go?" I asked.

"It doesn't matter. Just somewhere."

I backed out and took the first road that would point us out of town. When we were on the highway I pushed the truck to an easy 65 and let her coast. Fields and farms opened up in front of us. It was spring and the air crisp, the sky smudged with white dream clouds.

"Stop here," Joanie asked.

It was the first time either of us had spoken during the ride. I stopped the truck and she climbed out. I followed. When she saw the red-shouldered hawk circling, the same way Carl's used to do before he called it to his glove, she smiled and looked at me with soft eyes.

Even after the dozens of rides that we began taking together after Carl's death, she never failed to ask the same question. I always answered the same way, "Maybe it is. Maybe." Carl had always said that hawks were not like any other birds.

After the Party

It would have to be an Italian wine. That much was certain. What kind? Red? White? It hardly mattered, but it would almost surely be red. Red gave an air of sophistication, elegance, and a fair amount of importance to any situation, and the party next weekend would, without a doubt, be such an affair, as such parties tend to be, where people expect a dignified atmosphere. At least that's what most of them pretend to expect (not that they have any right to expect it in the first place), and so one must make a show of it – Merlot? Perhaps. Or, if one is feeling rather impish (he'd read about this once), some kind of Pinot.

The invitation had come in the mail the previous week and he received it eagerly. He never missed a party at their house if he could help it. Lots of food, wine by the case, of course, music, and a curious collection – some might say an odd assortment – of people, which theoretically never permitted a dull moment of conversation.

But something about it was different. It wasn't the invi-

tation itself that sparked his unease, but rather a pestering
condition in his chest that would surface, irritably, as if to
remind him that the sensation was close at hand, scratching the depths, and then it would subside briefly before
blooming again like a rash. He couldn't put his finger on its
cause at first. It was like the elusive dream on the brink of
sleep, mockingly, insolently out of reach.

It was the end of October. He would wear his heavy
coat, even take out the gloves for the first time this year.
And there it was, staring him down, October, four years
since the day Nancy left him. Getting older, but he still
went every year, like clockwork, whenever the invitations
came. But why did he go to these parties after all? he wondered. No one would have noticed if he stayed at home.
Red or white – did it matter? And if it didn't matter, then
why on earth did he insist on going? Time after time he
arrived at the door with a broad smile, pressing the doorbell with one hand, issuing a bottle of wine with the other,
an offering to please (or to appease?)... Whom? He didn't
know. An old man among couples half his age and avail-
able singles hoping to leave in twos.

The scene inside was always predictable down to the
smallest monotony (and the gaudy outfits – completely
unnecessary that costumes should be put on in the name
of sparking instant attraction). Of course, he could say this
now, in hindsight, but he too was once one of those young
boys fluffing his plumage years ago, chatting up many red

dresses and painted eyes, many names of which only one stayed with him for longer than one night.

Clusters gathered in each nook of the house. By open doors, along hallways, in side rooms. They held their glasses between thumb and forefinger and marked their space, stuck out their legs, propped elbows, rested hands on their hips. A few – and he usually found himself among them first – poked toothpicks into yellow and white cubes of cheddar or jack; then, maybe, a cherry tomato or two with dip and some sliced fruit. He liked the pineapple, but invariably someone took the big pieces, leaving him to scavenge the rest with no small displeasure.

What a way, he thought, to meet strangers, in a strange house hovering over a table full of cheese and cocktail wienies! But that part was bearable, it could be tolerated, even enjoyed if one tried. It was the rest of it that he could no longer stand, that which percolated inside him.

From the clusters of people, squibs of conversation would burst and echo once, maybe twice off the floor and walls – "Did she really sleep with him?" "I can't believe they lost, again. It's terrible." "So, how's work? The house? Good, that's good to hear." They bruised when they hit, and the bruises spread and overlapped like the night, gathering until they provided no escape from the darkness. The worst part was the realization that it wouldn't end until he too surrendered to the vortex of mortgages and mileage, ailments and inquiries after absent wives and friends.

"You know how he gets when he's talking computers," someone said in the distance, followed by a stiff palm plunging like a knife toward his middle, trailed by the words, "Hey, good running into you again." Hands were shaken, though the name had already faded from his memory like breath on cold glass. "How's your mother doing? Better?" "She's good, yes, yes she is," he said, wondering if it would have mattered if he'd said she'd taken a turn for the worse, found a faith healer she swore by, or died. Or if he just hadn't come – he'd be the absent one they inquired about. Maybe, maybe not. They'd stopped mentioning Nancy years ago, and he too could very well become a distant memory, just another one of the guests walking out the door and disappearing like so many disconnected voices.

The conversation and the evening continued to swirl toward midnight. "Hey, I heard you quit your old job! Geez, that must've been tough." "Yeah, I did, it was, it was terrible, but it's okay now." The pineapple gone, the wine gone, clusters were breaking form.

He shivered from the early morning chill as he walked toward the car. Too old for this, he thought, and another night headed home alone. October crept up his forearms and down his back still beaded in light sweat. He punched the radio off for the short drive home, becoming aware of the ringing in his ears after the last song escaped the stereo.

He pulled into the driveway, shut off the engine, stepped into the silent blacktop night. The ringing followed him through the screen door. He untied his shoes, placed them on the shoe rack, hung up his overcoat and the navy blazer bought specifically to match his pants. My God, had he really gone through all that trouble? Who did he think he would impress? The blonde law student who said she was working as a hygienist, a "dirty" job as she called it, until she could get a real job? Was that why he went these days? Did he become that guy that everyone whispers about from the corners of their mouths? No, no. He used to go with Nancy all the time. Now there simply was no Nancy. Nothing wrong with that. And yet nothing felt right since they'd stopped going together after the divorce. In those clusters and waves of perfumed voices one needs a buoy to keep from drowning, to not feel as if one is hopelessly lost at sea and going mad.

He sprawled out on the worn, brown leather couch, kicked up his feet and closed his eyes. Headlights played against the heavy backdrop of his eyelids.

"They'll come," he said to himself finally, eyes still closed. "They always do." They would come for the naked arms and the high-heeled legs, the right cologne, but they wouldn't say that of course. It wouldn't be polite. No one admits that's the real reason. It would sound more like, "Oh, thank you for having us, what a lovely kitchen," or

"We wouldn't miss it for anything. It's our pleasure to be here."

He knew better, had seen their eyes after a few glasses of wine, but he would plan a party nonetheless and invite all of them. The ones with the little black dresses and silver necklaces and the ones that came in jeans, just for the wine and free food. He liked them better. No pretense.

Because every month the same noose of friends gathered at a different house and November had yet to be claimed, he would host the party then.

He spent the next couple of weeks buying the necessary supplies. Color-coded napkins, paper plates, deluxe plastic forks and spoons, and extra matching wine glasses. The invitations were emailed the Monday before the party and by the end of the week most people had responded.

"You have a delightful house. It's so cozy," one said after the obligatory welcome tour. Just another way of saying "It's big, but not big enough." But tonight he wouldn't let things like that get to him. They were smiling and it was because of him. The food was good and there was plenty. Fresh pineapple everywhere. It was his party, after all. The music kept the conversation flowing without the need for shouting.

Not long after everyone arrived and the tours ended people started bunching up in threes and fours from the basement couch to the patio, concealed in a gauze of smoke drifting from mouth to mouth and spreading like fog across the ceiling. Talk trickled along the walls. The circles closed in again, limbs stiff and immovable, and he stepped farther away, clutching a half-empty glass. Where was that buoy? The room felt so crowded and so desolate. He shuffled by and snatched what he could of their words, piecing together what he knew but refused to admit, that only the place had changed. "Oh I know. I can't believe she comes to work wearing that. I mean, honestly." "He cashed out his 401K and gambled it away in less than an hour. Now he's got nothing." "Maybe I need more wine."

The clusters broke once more and dissipated out the door into the night, engines starting in the darkness up and down the block. Thank yous sifted through the screen. "We had a wonderful…" "We should do this again…" One by one they left and the music gave way to vacant rooms, echoes of ice in empty glasses, a crisp, fragrant late autumn night. When everyone had departed, there was a faint ringing that remained in his ears. They had come, as they always did, and left the same way. He put out the lights of dying candles with several quick puffs, those last bursts of color playing over and over in his mind as he lay down to sleep.

Used Pencil Store

The used pencil store owner was dusting one of the displays when I walked in. It smelled of wood shavings and small piles were pitched against the walls.

"Each one is hand sharpened," I heard him say, still with his back turned to me and running a duster along an empty shelf above his head.

I picked up the first thing that drew my attention, a yellow No. 2, maybe half worn. Hexagonal shaft, silver eraser cup, eraser a bit too dry. You can tell these things. If you scratch the eraser head lightly with your thumbnail and the color underneath is significantly lighter than that of the surface then chances are the eraser has dried out from disuse or simply the passage of time. It would leave smudges of pink on paper if you tried to make something disappear.

"You won't find any mechanical pencils, if that's what you're looking for. No sir. Wood and lead. All wood. Solid. I make sure of that."

Some of the displays had pencils sticking out of small coffee cans, erasers pointing down so as not to blunt the tips. Some were lined up along the counter and on top of a few small tables, all of the tips pointing in the same direction.

"Do you have any colored pencils?" I asked.

"No sir. No colored pencils. Hard to come by. Hard to keep a steady supply."

Some of the pencils were so worn down they were no bigger than stubs, impossible to hold in your hand, much less do any writing. I lifted up a blue one that had some ornate characters along the shaft in bright red paint, almost cheerful. I thought it had a well-executed balance between functionality and style. I held it up in his direction (he'd turned by now and was following me with his eyes as I went around the room) as if to say "Tell me about this." Nothing in the store had a label of any sort besides what was written on the pencils and even most of those were so badly scuffed and worn that they were illegible.

"Just came in, that one," he said. "Soft lead. Very unusual. The writing is smooth but it lacks some of the control along the page you get with some other models. If you're looking for a workhorse, this here..."

I really wasn't interested and let his voice trail off as I kept pacing the room. Some displays were arranged according to what I deduced to be prior history. One display had six pencils, all with round shafts, pure cylinders. All suffered at one time severe teeth marks. Some only a few nervous bites I assumed, but others bore indentations so deep and dense that could only have been caused by frequent, deliberate chewing. I lifted up the one that seemed most abused and held it up to the light, not necessarily to see it any better but because that's just the kind of thing you do with objects you're in awe of and can't put down for fear of losing them or causing harm.

I brought it with me gently to the counter. It was a lot less than what I expected. The shopkeeper took the pencil in his left hand and arranged the tip between thumb and forefinger. With his right hand he grabbed a whittling knife and began chipping off the wood and letting it fall to the ground. When he was done he placed the pencil inside a small paper bag. He licked the tip of his own pencil and wrote out a receipt, which he also placed in the bag. We exchanged no other words, and with the end of the ritual I took the bag and exited the store.

That night at home I took it out and again held it to the light. I smelled the wood and ran my fingers along the indentations, imagining the boy or girl slumped over some exam they struggled to finish or some homework problem seemingly without answer. Their mouths were wrapped around that pencil and the teeth sunk into the wood with a gentle crushing sound and they kept turning that pencil and drilling more holes into it keeping the sound somewhere deep inside the chest. Maybe their lips and their tongues and their teeth were also a bit dirty with a wet gray from the lead, their papers smudged with a handwriting not yet their own. And for the first time that day I did what I knew I wanted to do ever since I walked through the door of that used pencil shop. I placed it in my mouth, held on to the end with the eraser with my right hand, and bit down as hard as I could.

Beginnings

On late afternoons it's not uncommon for me to sit out on the open porch and wish for the sky to blacken prematurely over the red tiled rooftops, wish for it to bring its heavy sigh under which all other sighs would be swept. One sound to swallow up all of the other sounds. But today the weather no longer seems to resemble itself. On top of the house the metal bird is being turned this way and that, making me dizzy just looking at it, the wild screech as it spins getting caught in the wind pulling another one from its throat to unsettle the silence. I welcome what it might bring because there is no alternative. The weather makes no distinction among beasts, be clear on that. It beats the fields flat, it burns through a year's worth of dry hope just to give you pause, a reason to stand still and do nothing but watch in blind horror. It knows that it was born on the wrong side of the blame game, despite what old men might be inclined to whisper on their knees on Sunday before the almighty.

In a small upstate New York town I knew a man only by his house: his existence was tied to that place and nothing more. The numbers on the house hung upside down and backwards, meaning and significance long ago claimed by the rust. When he died, as is the case with all small-town news, the local paper published an inventory of unclaimed possessions: a pair of boots and one very good kitchen knife. Below that, there was an ad for imported shaving cream featuring the word *essence* or *extract*, I forget which. Days before, former lovers and the remainders of family had come through and picked at the insides behind covered windows. They took everything except the boots and the knife. The townsfolk would be talking about that for years. *Think about it*, they would say, *only one good knife*, as they bent over piles of dirty dishes, as they chopped their garlic and onions, but still couldn't manage to cry for him.

I planned to propose to her on the same day as the anniversary of my parents' engagement. I'm sure in my mind it was rather symbolic. The number of people who knew about us was insignificant and I liked that. To keep a secret you have to make people believe that they already know what the secret is. Out of some outmoded sense of decorum everyone keeps their silence, each one confident in the knowledge that they are the only ones. Of course, it wasn't an outright lie, just a pervasive sense of vagueness that allows the curious and the not-so-innocent to fabricate the answers they can live with. Such is the lifeline, the lifeblood of a village. It must give the appearance that everything is known about everyone even though fences are the first to rise up out of the dirt and the doors almost always remain closed. At times we all need validation that we still exist.

Our courtship had been a quick one. We met, became engaged, and said our vows all within a year. The first months of dating were passionate, filled with almost animal desires. When we were together it felt as if we'd been reunited after years of being apart. The whole sweaty palms and butterflies routine. When we had to separate for a while, the goodbyes were prolonged and difficult, and I would always find something to keep me busy, to fill the gap of time between visits, before seeing her again.

I used to come home from the university and do the same thing every day. Got out of my car, pressed the button on the remote twice just to be sure – *beep beep, beep beep.* That was New York still scratching under my skin. Then I checked my mailbox and went upstairs and sometimes I ran into the widow who lives in the apartment below me. She talked to me while I held two bags of groceries in both hands, my fingers slowly getting numb, but I didn't interrupt.

In this chair, at this table, here watching sky and movement, I feel painfully nostalgic for the future. Not some distant, unimaginable future, but the very next breath, the getting to the bottom of a good cup of coffee. I feel an overwhelming sense of pleasure and sadness imagining that first drop of rain plummeting through the heat following its shadow until it hits the ground and hops back up in pieces. I feel the same about walking along the outside of the fence after the storm passes to see if any of the flowers I planted there are still standing. If not, I will carry them with me to the cemetery when the ground has had time to dry.

When I say that the weather no longer resembles itself I think that's what makes it more like it should be. I've got no business thinking that it should look one way or the other. When I have time to go and see the girl a few streets down I listen and I learn things like that, things I've always known. I would tell you her name but I don't call her by her name. No one in the village calls another by their name. At first it was something that bothered me but eventually I came to appreciate the sheer genius and efficiency of it. If you could be traced down the family line to the lost soul who put down roots here generations ago then your name is fixed in the common imagination of the village, much like its own name, and you don't really have a say in it. You're simply great grandson of X or wife of the great grandson of X or the daughter of the son of X, and so on. You even start to refer to yourself by that title when people inquire and there's a sense of pride that goes into that, an acknowledgement that you stand for more than yourself.

I, great great grandson of X, am watching the sky and I am paralyzed with nostalgia. Tomorrow I could stop by and see her and we would talk for some time (I can even build the entire conversation in my head) but eventually it would come to an end, and I envision the walk back as dusk settles in being filled with the sorrow of something beautiful being gone, of starting over, again and again, always remembering what was and what will be.

Spain in summertime when Clare and I became inseparable, temporarily. We met there for the first time even though we lived less than five blocks from each other in the city. Clare stayed on the floor below me at the house, and we saw each other only briefly during the day. We claimed to be there for work. Clare was researching a book on the history of street theater. I started something that I never finished, resisting the urge to write her into the story, a bad habit I'd acquired long ago.

We spent our nights in town, in that surreal comfort that comes from knowing it's only a summer romance. Everyone seemed to be making up their own reality as they went along. We went for dinner, coffee, shows. We commented on the wine as if we knew what we were talking about, using words like vintage, palate, legs, and oaky. Sometimes we smoked afterward while the evening wound down toward the clear bottom of another long-necked bottle. Other times we would wander into late-night cafes and bars. We drowned ourselves in the thick smoke of it. We sat and watched the people in perfunctory conversations, saw and heard them pour out their life stories as if it mattered beyond the next hour.

I used to tell myself that when I got back to New York the first thing I would do is go to a diner, one of the old fashioned ones, a railroad car by the side of the road, one that looks like it's been around since before you were born. Greek owner, naturally, a Mexican or some other South American at the grill and another in the back scrubbing the dishes. Somewhere up north, beyond the Pennsylvania line. I would sit down at a vinyl booth, some gaudy color scratched and taped up over the years, and I want to be served by some waitress who calls everyone "Honey" or

"Sugar" no matter if they're ten years old or eighty. The coffee would be watered down, there would be paper place mats with advertisements of local hardware stores, land-scaping, even the funeral parlor down the street. I would order eggs, bacon, home fries, and toast. You can always tell a good diner by its home fries. Not the eggs. Eggs are eggs, if they're natural, and not the kind that come pre-scram-bled in a container. You crack them over the grill, rough 'em up with the edge of the spatula and you're done. But the home fries are a different story altogether. They can be cut into small cubes or large chunks. They can be soft or crispy. Depending on the cook you'll get them perfect-ly seasoned or a non-descript sloppy mound on your oth-erwise perfect plate. One taste of the home fries and you know it's the right place. That's the first thing I would do if I got back to the city.

I flew from New York to San Francisco for a promotion. Whenever she knew that I would be leaving she would broach the subject several days before. She dreaded the time during which we would be separated. To me it made no difference. I would be back soon.

"It'll be fine. I'm only gone for four days," which I knew was the wrong thing to say, but it made sense to me. To her it meant that I didn't take the time to consider the possibility that I would feel her absence. I thought I meant that four days isn't really all that long in the big scheme of things.

I look out over the land looking back over me from head to toe like some alien particle that doesn't quite fit its cosmology. And the dirt in my hair, and the dirt in my eyes, and the pump grease on my hands that the hard well water won't wash away so easily – all of that and still no more than a dirty, dusty heap of a man weighing on and willing for something, anything to keep me in its memory.

No, we did not have a reservation. And with that, the hostess stared right past me through the large glass windows that looked onto the sidewalk and the night that had fallen swiftly over the town. We walked out into the street and the summer was sweet and warm in the air. From one end of the street we could hear a piano and a saxophone, from the other end a cover band trying to bring the dead back to life. Cars rolled up, someone got in or out, and the cars rolled right on by in a constant stream of lights and storefront reflections, the glint of metal and exhaust that hung like breath and was replaced by more cars and the same, on and on. My girl and I walked holding hands between other couples holding hands or pushing strollers, eating ice cream from paper cups with miniature plastic spoons, and I couldn't help thinking just then how like miniatures all of us must look from above in the great Midwestern sky that stretched above us. We'd forgotten about the restaurant soon enough. It wasn't for us, anyway, Katya assured me. We stopped at a store and picked up some meat and a bag of onions and some wine. We went back to the apartment. I threw the meat into a pan and sliced up the onions. I stuck the wine bottle between my knees and pulled at the cork until it slipped out with a loud pop that resonated in the emptiness. We ate the meat that night with the cooked onions and salt and drank the wine from coffee cups. We sat on the floor. That's how we spent most nights that summer. We had no furniture yet, no table or chairs or sofa, just a few bed sheets and pillows we folded together the best way we could. I had just gotten a teaching job at the local university and in just a few days I had packed everything I owned and left the East Coast for the Midwest and the promise of steady work. Most people said, "take it…", "in these times…", "don't be stupid…", and other such things, common things. So I sold what I could, gave away what I couldn't and packed the rest in a truck and drove it West across the country, through Pennsylvania, Ohio, Indiana, a flat landscape of sky and earth, one long, interminable horizon you could never reach. Katya tagged along for a while, vacation, until she had to return back East and I would be left to the apartment and the sounds of the nearby highway whistling and grinding by on its way somewhere through the darkness.

We ate together on the floor and took it for the way things were going to be. We fried meat in the pan and drank cheap cabernet. We listened to the same jazz CD over and over. Every night we would put on that record and by the end of it we would almost be done with the bottle and each night we grew more sick of the music and each night we put it back on and listened to it like we were hearing it for the first time. When we were in town we got by with as little as we could. We became experts at window shopping, trying on hats and dresses in second hand stores with their musty smells and old fashioned handwritten labels that reminded me of the way my grandfather used to write letters long ago before he couldn't write anymore because there were no more things to do, there was no more to say. Sometimes we would get an ice cream cone and we would share it down by the river that ran east and west through the little town, the north and south of its streets making little bridges for lovers to stop and take a picture and move on or linger for a few minutes not saying anything, just looking at the lazy water in no hurry to get anywhere. Sometimes, when it was too hot to do much of anything, we went to a nearby lake that had a patch of sand and grass and we spread a blanket and sat there under the weather until we grew hot and had to wade into the water to cool down. Most days went by like that, with nothing really to show for it in the end, and if someone asked me what else I would rather be doing, well, I didn't really want to do anything else. Something happened that summer but I couldn't tell you exactly how it was that it happened, when and where, or any of the other specifics of this general feeling that came to define most of my thoughts and musings on things. One thing I knew was that I was done running, chasing something that had been dangled in front of me like a ghost only to disappear when I got close enough to reach out my hand. Katya never mentioned it, but she sensed something had changed and just went with it, which I was thankful for because I had no real explanation and in fact it didn't really make much sense in the way that most things don't really make sense when pricked and prodded, but from a distance they just seem right and honest and as natural as breathing in and out. And even that can make you feel strange if you stop and think about it, if you pause to count every breath and feel the tension in your muscles as the chest fills and empties with air until you lose count and forget yourself again, forget that you are this living thing passing among other living and dead things at all hours of the day, exchanging words and looks and money across counters, the short goodbyes at the end of a long night. We passed like that ourselves, like the night air between buildings and cars and the women out keeping up with their men who liked to walk just a few steps ahead, just enough to be in front, which is the way it is I suppose, since most people don't really think about where they are, only how fast or how slow they are going.

When we talked on the phone she would ask often:

"How was your day?"

"Fine," I'd say.

"What did you do?"

"Not much."

"Do you miss me?"

"Why do you always ask that?"

"I shouldn't have to ask."

"Then don't."

"Do you?"

She was getting irritated.

"Do I what?"

"Miss me."

"Sure. You know that."

"But you never say it."

I knew I never said it.

"I wish you'd say it sometimes without me having to ask for it."

I missed her. I just didn't think about it or say it. When I was alone I didn't find it difficult to keep myself occupied with my own thoughts or whatever I had planned for the day. After all, that's what I had been doing and doing well since before we'd met. She would not understand if she ever knew that she was not vital to my existence, that she did not make up the air I breathed, that if she were no longer there I would still be able to go on.

Katya put on her dress at night and it didn't matter that she only had one pair of shoes because she had a pair of legs that made you forget about the shoes, and she walked with her shoulders pushed back just a bit, her bare neck tall and white in the lingering heat. We stood out in that place or I felt like we did, which in the end is the same thing. The older women were brown and wrinkled from too much sun and the younger women were all beautiful blondes squeezed into short skirts on impossible heels, except for the ones who were not so beautiful, too fat or too skinny, and they drank too much by themselves but still squeezed into short skirts and impossible heels because it seemed like the right thing to do. The men were mostly tall and plain. They were khakis-and-a-blue-dress-shirt sort of men. Some had sweaters with tiny logos. They wore loafers with tassels that jiggled when they walked. The boys did not tuck in their shirts but they were also blue. The night we went to the restaurant the two of us looked good together. I had tucked in my shirt, my shoes were black, there were empty tables, we didn't have reservations. That was the situation. A few weeks after that I was to start my new job. I had a new office, a new chair, my name on a plate screwed to the wall. A tree shook in the breeze outside my window. The first paycheck was still weeks away. We ate meat and onions some more, listened to jazz with our feet tucked under us and then fell asleep together, thinking about doing things. Maybe that summer I realized that all I ever wanted was to see things and do things and talk about them with someone else who also just wants to see and do things. But I'm not sure that's possible anymore. There's too much of the world and it asks of us, it always asks, that by the end we've nothing left to give or take with us wherever we go. We're hollow, which sounds trite, I know I know, but look at it this way. Think of it as an Indian Summer. We fool ourselves when it goes on longer than it should although we know it's not the way things really are and we call it a blessing anyway. We could have the small things, we tell ourselves. That's a lie. We fall asleep full of the small lies we swallow.

The best way to learn how to lie is to listen to those who preach honesty. It takes longer than it should to realize this. No one who says "be honest" really wants to hear what honesty really sounds like. When someone asks me "How do you like it here?" I tell them what they want to hear. It's a kind of truth, even if it doesn't mean anything.

I lay down a couple sheets of newspaper and sit Indian style on the bare kitchen floor to prepare to shine my boots. I wipe the boots clean with a damp rag and dry the boots before dipping the brush in the polish and applying it in circles across the surface of the boot, working it into the leather until it is all covered in black, and it is this doing that fascinates me the most. How I remember learning the right way to guide the brush from my grandpa sitting on this or that kitchen floor, how my hands and my arms move now with a rhythm it took practice to build, more circles across the leather with a worn rag in one hand, the other splayed inside the boot as a rack so I could hold it up to the lamp to see if I've missed a spot. Then with a wide, clean brush I begin adding the shine, stroke by stroke, again my mind fixed on the doing of it, the motion I couldn't get just right as a boy because maybe my muscles had never had to work that way before and maybe my eyes had never seen a hand move that way before, and now on the floor alone the boots a midnight black picking up light, my fingers smelling of leather and polish, hands begin gathering up tools.

In San Francisco I stayed with friends who'd done well for themselves. The girl had laid out the table and when dinner was finished she came to pick up the plates and take them to the kitchen. She was young and delicate, with long arms and legs, a narrow face with even more delicate features. They said her name was Sam. She moved from task to task without much expression.

Katya is always excited. She is happy, genuinely happy. I envy her. I say that I can't work like I used to. She tells me that the thing in itself is what kills. Absolutes. A kind of personal religion. Then we talk weather and Indian summers. Somehow I get on the topic of politics and money. Always money and how the job I thought would make it easier just makes it more obvious how far we are from anything like happiness. When we sit down to dinner I am grateful for her presence and for the food. I think free trade agreements, open markets, the exploitation of nations that have even less than we do. I imagine that in South America they're just beginning to rise as we sit across from each other in the still dark hours of a new day, our elbows so close that I could smell the grapefruit and cinnamon on her skin. I'm grateful for that, the light reflecting in her blue eyes, that man living in a country we will never see, the dirt and the rain he brings with him to bed each night. The way he lies down with his wife to make love as if there's nothing else to lose, no need to mask what's really on their minds with the weight of perfumed secrets, the silence of

December's falling snow, those nights that never truly disappear without a trace. And just like that Katya goes back to the weather, the way the trees are green and full of life or yellow and red and full of life. Everything is full of life for her. She goes for walks and thinks about nothing. She is not dead. She is the solid line I use as my guide.

By the end of summer I learned that few things meant more to Clare than the theater. And that, of course, included me. Her appetite for it, for performance, bordered on the obsessive. When the curtain was raised she became lost in her own world, naked, oblivious. The same if she found herself in the audience. She would sit there mesmerized, forgetting herself, forgetting about me. I drank for both of us.

Sam was in the kitchen rinsing the plates. She had her back to me, but she heard the door as I walked in and turned to look over her shoulder. Her hair fell over her eyes. I paused in the middle of the room before going to the fridge.

I introduced myself even though I wasn't asked.

"I know. I've seen your books," she said.

"Oh," I said, and I knew that I sounded surprised. "So, you like them?"

"I haven't read them. There were some copies lying around before you got here."

I didn't have a response. It wasn't what I'd expected to hear.

"How long have you worked here?"

"Three months," she said, again over her shoulder, hair moist with sweat.

She was probably much younger than me but she didn't look it. Or maybe it was that I've been told I don't look as old as I really am. Whatever the case, it pleased me to think about it. I finished getting some ice from the freezer and left the room.

The evening wound down, I excused myself, claiming a tiresome plane ride, and went to my room. There was a message from Karen on my phone wishing me a good rest. That night I thought of Sam before falling asleep.

The next day I read in front of a decent crowd and scrawled a few pages with my incomprehensible name. Karen called to ask how it went. She was always the one to call. It went well, I told her. She sounded like she was bored alone, and said she wished that I were there with her. I said I'd be there soon.

At the university I worked with a woman who was promoted twice in one year. Every time she got a promotion her title changed, and I imagine the boxes of business cards getting tossed out each time, names and address-es and numbers meaningless now without something to hold on to.

I would be in San Francisco for two more days. On Sunday my hosts had planned a tour of some galleries. We admired the artwork on the walls, talking in whispers the way people tend to do in galleries and white-hushed spaces. Strolling door-to-door gave me something else to think about, to keep my mind busy.

At dinnertime whenever Sam came through the door I glanced in her direction. I was aware that I was doing it and feared that others at the table might notice as well. But no one paid attention. They were all busy picking at the food in front of them, turning to each other with affected gestures whenever someone said anything, however ordinary. It was the polite thing to do. I kept up with them the best I could. I endured the exercise in dividing my attention between those who wanted it and the girl who moved in and out of their circle yet remained unaffected by it. I realized that my mind was occupied with her although I didn't understand why. I couldn't make sense of her.

A few years ago they put a payphone on the corner of my street and the main road. It had one of those plastic red casings that made it look like some futuristic space pod that attached itself artificially and with bad intentions onto a fence. Among the wood and weeds and sour cherry trees it stood out like a sore thumb. I imagine someone going out there, standing by themselves linked by a cord to a payphone trying to reach the other side of the world, or the city an hour away, which might as well be the same thing. It didn't last long. Only the plastic shell remains bolted to the wooden fence on the corner, the phone itself gone, another relic, another reminder of what was. Now the sheepherders, the gimp's son and the one with the twitch on the left side of his face, lean on their walking sticks with one hand, the other holding a mobile phone. We are all connected in this new game with a new name and a set of rules that no one even knows yet.

Eventually the furniture arrived at the apartment one piece at a time. We put it together and found empty places for it. The empty room was no longer empty. It started to look like every other apartment where a man would live with a woman who knows what she wants. It had an arrangement that was pleasing to the eye. We even picked out a table but brought it back to the store the next day with some trumped up story about quality and workmanship. The truth was that we had gotten used to the floor and the dull gray carpet, the way we were closer on the floor than we would ever be across a table, poised on two wooden chairs with two more that would never be used because they tell you to take them, don't be stupid, just in case. I guess we were stupid. But now we had more money left over for the wine. And books. Lots of books all over the floor, the kitchen counter and the mantle, lined up or stacked, straight or crooked, books with stories and poems, and books about books. I'll admit that we never read most of them, but we made plans.

The university would be in session soon so we began to prepare for the day Katya would head back to New York. She had one bag. I drove her to the airport and she got on a plane and a few hours later she was back home and out of the lazy Midwestern summer. I arranged my office and awaited the beginning of the year and I didn't know why or for what reason. I went out at night just to walk through the sidewalk music, the smell of it and the voices that no longer made any sense to me. Everything was all color and darkness under a wide westward sky that appeared, like us, to be at a crossroads, terrifying and infinite.

When Labor Day rolled around I was terribly lonely. Concerts in the park under the lights, children running and circling the same patch of green grass. They were screaming their childhoods under the big sky and no one listened. On some days there were street fairs and carnivals with Italian sausage carts, fried dough and powdered sugar, cotton candy, and a dozen other sweets, beer tents, beer that flowed as if it would never end. And street musicians, the good and the bad, I heard them all. I saw the street sweepers and the taxi drivers idling on corners. Every day I saw this and every night a part of me died. I had longed for this since I was a child, told myself this would be a kind of life, and there I was, in the perfect summer of tailor-made lawns and rows of trees in full bloom. And it was too late. In that town, in that apartment, something in me was ever lonelier. Somehow I knew everything was beautiful, beautiful and strange. I kept frying meat in the pan, bought bags of apples and ate them cut up with honey and cinnamon. I wanted it to be like home, like the holidays when everything smells of cinnamon and you wake into it with sleepy eyes but smile because it means another day of sweet air and cinnamon. I wanted it to be like that and it wasn't.

Clare wrote plays that were performed in small venues all over the city. She had fans that followed her work and showed up to shows. She had reviews in the papers. People would come up to her at times and say things like, "I love your work" or "So honest, such passion." Those things made her happy.

She told me once, more as a way of making herself believe it, that when she worked on a play she lived in a world few others would ever understand entirely. She made something special and because of that she became more than herself. How could they see that? Hours at a time she lived her life a notch above the ordinary.

And then it passed. All of it wrong. Wrong. Wrong. Wrong. Not good enough. Not what it could've been.

By spring I had a car. It had a dent on the passenger side and a side mirror that didn't match. I would get in the car and drive through the suburbs that managed to live up to the clichéd monotony of architecture and streets, beautifully coiffed laws and shrubs, the whole 1950s American dream. I drove straight through sometimes until I reached the limits of the city, past the last empty lot that bled into a barren field stretching beyond anything I could see. It would be dark and the lights back in the direction I came from seemed lost under the immensity of night. Another mile and another world – the poor side of town. Run down, dirty, the other America. I'd seen it before in New York, in the neighborhoods where I grew up. It smelled like that. Like younger days when the hours are a struggle from morning until the last light goes off and you know you're just going to sleep so you can do it all over. I started smoking again. I bought whatever was cheaper. One day I stepped outside the café where I'd been working to have a cigarette and to stretch my legs. A girl came out for a cigarette and I let her borrow my lighter. She asked what I was smoking and I told her. She said, "those taste like poverty," and she didn't say anything else. I said nothing else.

Karen called to say goodnight. We had to say goodnight each day I was away, otherwise I knew it would upset her. We talked about the same things we always talked about. It had gotten predictable to a degree, but tonight I realized that I was feeling more talkative. I wanted her to think that everything was going on as it usually did when I was away, and for the most part it was. But one thought kept nagging me. It tormented me to know that she might suspect my thoughts. Not out of shame, but because she would be hurt by them. Because my thoughts that night were focused on someone else.

The initial step was to clear the land of months of disuse, the shrubs, crabgrass, the dandelions, you name it. First lesson – everything has consequences you have to be able to foresee, a matter of basic survival among men. It would seem to be common sense, but the things you would never give a second thought to take on added significance here. With wheelbarrows full of weeds on hand the only option was to burn them or take them far enough outside the village and dump them by the side of the road. I chose the former. I knew enough to make small piles around the yard and let them dry for several days. When I felt they were dry enough and ready to burn I piled them together outside in the street, poured on the gasoline and set the whole mess on fire. As luck would have it much of it only looked dry when it was still very much green on the inside, which created a great deal of smoke for several hours. A neighbor came to complain over the fence. I tried to ignore his words and gestures, and I raised my shoulders as if to say "what can I do?" but I knew the day's meaning as soon as I saw the white cotton plume rise from the pile of grass – you have much to learn; what you think you know won't get you far here; you don't get many second chances.

Learning a country life. The land cleared, the weeds finally burned, I started working from morning till night, shovel and hoe in hand. I kept at it all day, kept at it until it felt good, the wooden handles in my hand, the sound of a sharp blade cutting through the soil, that pleasurable pain that travels the body and seems to fill every muscle with purpose. The sun above, the breeze drying the sweat on your shoulders, the day that is wholly your own to do with as you will. All that, day after day for a week straight, and barely a dent made. I'd broken my back, blistered and burned my skin, and the land still toyed with me, still claimed its rights over me.

Hard work takes time. It is made up of time and the muscle behind it is incidental. It takes knowing when and how. It is and it is not brute force. It is all about using what little you have to get the most out of it. To survive here is an act of will. I wake up mornings and I can barely hold the handle of the coffee pot over the flame. My fingers ache until they loosen again and remember their purpose.

One morning I woke up and opened the front gate and she was standing there staring at me wagging her auburn tail. I threw some food into the grass and closed the gate. The next morning she was there again. This time I left the gate open and she followed me in. I let her eat what I had out on the veranda then motioned that it was time for her to leave, I had work to do. She lay down and looked up at me from the ground, not moving a muscle, just watching me with big black eyes. She could tell me some things I thought. I noticed the wide gashes in her fur. The dried mud on her paws. The clumps of thistle that she couldn't reach to bite off. I named her Lola.

I have three dogs now. Two girls and one boy that walks with a limp. If he sits down for too long his muscles tense up and he has trouble moving. On cold mornings I have to rub his haunches to get the blood flowing and loosen the joints so he could go about his business. I know I'll get like that soon enough. I see myself in him, the silent acceptance that that's how it is and that it won't change, moving through the hours of a day because that's what is being asked of you by some instinct as awful or beautiful as it is necessary. And sometimes when he and I sit for too long Lola comes along and nudges him, thrusts her nose under my palm and says let's go let's play let's do something, and I sigh and I get up and I go in the direction she's leading me.

Our dinner conversations kept the world at bay, that all-too-common world of false starts and rude interruptions. And when it was all over we shared her room until morning. Clare liked to wind down watching television. I liked to go to bed, feeling her body stretch itself against mine under the covers. Sometimes I'd wake up in the middle of the night and notice that she wasn't there. I would go into the living room to find her still awake on the couch, staring at the televised screen and curtains, the volume off, tears down her face. I would wipe her tears and kiss her forehead, then turn off the television and walk her to bed. More tears would dry out on my chest before she fell asleep to God knows what dark corners she retreated in her dreams.

How to explain the pleasure of talking to a girl on the other side of a fence. The apricots fragrant overhead, the splintered wood rough against your palm pressing closer. And her face jutting in and out of view between the uneven slats, mingling with sunlight, the flower arrangement on the outdoor table, a dress with modest colors. And the conversation as it should be when it's well past noon and the air is lazy, the animals too, and even the words fall victim to the heat. She asks, where were you yesterday? I say I was out in the yard, working, as if it were something new, some big proud accomplishment. She turns and rings out the water from a rag and says nothing. She clothes pins the rag to a line of electrical wire that runs from the eaves to a tree in the middle of the garden. And the garden is heavy with a bit of everything and I try to recognize all of the smells but I can't separate them, they're all one big country smell and in my head when I leave heading home she smells of that same smell, vegetable sweet, dirt dry, clean as air off the lake. I ask her if she ever goes into town. She says yes, sometimes. A few days earlier I learned that her father puts the classical radio station on all day from morning until it is time for bed. The only time the music is not playing is if there's a game on and the national team is playing and that's when work stops to cheer on the boys. She lists some of her favorite composers. A few times she's been to the city to hear the philharmonic. I tell her I used to come here to get away from the city. She says nothing as if it's obvious or it doesn't matter or she doesn't care or all of that and goes about cutting something up on the table, wiping her forehead with her sleeve. Before I leave she says her father is going fishing on Saturday. He goes fishing every Saturday.

The hard lines we will dare one another to cross are still a mystery as the day we were born without shame. We smooth them out with the softest petal veins but it is never the same – every word become rigid and certain.

And when the morning light clears the air between us it is with nothing but time. Where you would expect a sufficient parting, the open hand baffles and reaches beyond its shore, unfolding like a wave, then turning back so that it might be followed.

In New York, Clare wrote in spite of yourself. It was all struggle and release and back to the struggle. No surprise that in another country she felt at home in a way that she hadn't felt in a long time. It was exactly what it could never be in a place where they know you – one big show with no one to judge and no pressure to perform for anyone but herself. The open doors had invited us in, plied us with their food and drink, but we always stayed for after-hours theater – the music, the lights, the characters that pumped new life into the night.

I met Katya in a local bar past midnight, a place for the regulars, mostly men sitting on stools at the bar looking like they would know every knot and crack in the surface of the counter. They swiveled part way toward the door as I entered. They swiveled back to ball game highlights on the television lodged above the bar. I got a drink and looked around. One pool table angled in a corner. Two men and a woman were playing. That was Katya. She was tallish, but not lanky. The three of them took turns slapping the pool balls with a single house cue, not really playing anything that required a strict adherence to rules, not really aiming for the pockets with a desire to sink the shot, just a distraction to break up the silence between bursts of conversation. "So you need to get drunk to do it?" Katya asked. "Yea. Pretty much. I sleep in as late as I can, I wake up, have a drink, paint, drink some more, paint, etc.," the man said, a nervous tic making his glasses shift up and down on the bridge of his nose as he talked. His voice was measured, its cadence giving off the impression of self-assuredness. He spoke with his whole body, the outstretched fingers of his hands like claws trying to mold meaning out of the air or otherwise wrench some kind of sense out of it. The other man with them remained silent, looking back and forth between Katya and the painter. He held the cue in both hands and propped the fat end into the floor as he listened to the explanation. He pressed his weight against it as if it were a walking stick. He could have been a character in any of the country songs that were playing overhead, whittling his life away in the dim barroom light of a place that seemed made specifically for such a purpose. Something about him made me feel jealous but I didn't know that back then. "Well, I think that's stupid," I heard Katya say. "You could paint without drinking, can't you?" He looked at his drink and said, "Well, yes, I could, I suppose. But it's just not the same." I got a good look at her as she turned away from him. My first thought was *she's very proportionate*. I heard the other man call out after her, "It's no use, Katya. I've tried. He wants to be famous when he dies." That's how I learned her name.

The village was named in honor or fear of a wild animal. Without choice the people wear that ghost-name, suffering its skeletons both dead and walking. The animal itself hasn't been seen in these parts for generations. Some hate the name and some claim it with pride. Call it what you will I guess – both the curse and the blessing of lineage. But because I'm not a confirmed believer I err on the side of whatever gives the moment its color, just enough indecision not to invite any more unwanted grief. That I have a knack of building up on my own.

I found reason to excuse myself and went to the kitchen. Sam sat on a stool next to the counter, placing sliced strawberries in a symmetric pattern on top of the cake she was about to bring to the table. She looked up and smiled.

"Great meal," I said.

"Thank you," was all she said.

"Is Sam short for something?"

"Samantha," she replied. I knew she'd heard that question a million times.

I watched as her fingers handled the strawberries as if she were placing tiles on a mosaic. My eyes followed her bare arms up to the rolled up sleeves toward the long, thin neck and her collarbone exposed by two buttons undone. I realized that I'd been standing there without saying anything for some time as Samantha continued preparing the platter. I wanted her at that moment, my body yearned to touch hers, and I wanted to say so, but resisted the temptation. I said instead, "I'm looking forward to dessert."

She looked up and our eyes met. I knew I was making too much out of a single look. I wasn't thinking clearly. I was a married man with a wife many others would jump at the chance to be with. And she loved me. Why couldn't I do the same? This girl, this young woman with a wisp of a body had barely shared more than a passing glance and polite conversation with me because that was her job. She didn't mean anything. I desperately wanted to assure myself with that last thought.

I walked back into the dining room, my body tense

with the sensation of something unfulfilled. Sam brought out the dessert. When she leaned over my shoulder to hand me my plate I smelled the subtle perfume of her skin.

I keep finding myself wishing for rain. Not exactly a prayer, but a kind of longing I make known with my silence. I need it to keep me in, to keep everybody in, to give us something to talk about the next day. And it always does. There's either too little or too much of it. In which case I push the rain out with a broom and I stand in the doorway still thinking nothing but the rain.

The village happened to be stuck between two larger towns. When a road was needed to connect larger town A and larger town B, everyone welcomed progress. Knock down a couple of houses, raze part of the forest, same with the fields. The concrete slabs came over on giant rigs and were laid down end-to-end, kilometer after kilometer. A pale gray band winding between the houses. When a truck rumbled through it announced its roar as it echoed in the valley, it shook the walls of the houses, it left behind a cloud of dust that fell back down over everything in sight, turning the green grass to dust, the trees to dust, the air into more dust.

One day we happened to be on opposite sides of the

road, she going off on an errand and me coming back with a few bags of my own. A truck sped between us and she became only a blur on the other side. She waved her hand in front of her face to clear the dust, scrunching her nose, and made a sign as if to say, "I have to go."

If there had been no road between us maybe she would have waited and I would have asked her what she was going to buy. I would have told her that I needed parts for the pump and that's where I had been.

I left Spain at the end of July to go back home, and she stayed for a few more weeks. We exchanged letters irregularly afterwards. When she returned to New York we saw each other a few times, but there wasn't any false pretense that it would ever be more than that. We went to a show together. She told me she found a publisher for her book but she didn't talk about it. It was just an exercise in a second-rate skill, making a living. My own piece was still in parts.

Clare moved up north shortly after, got out of the city and bought a house. The last night of her final play filled in seats with those who had come to say goodbye. When she wrote, she never mentioned the nights at the cafes and she didn't really need to. Sitting by myself in the dim light of a bar it was all I could think about, although I never said so either. We sent variations of vague how-are-you letters almost out of obligation. If it became more than that I don't think I could deal with the guilt or the self-pity. Which of us came out on the losing end? Did either of us win? We suffered our own betrayals in silence – hoping, maybe, for another blossom in the smallest heartache.

I went to my room to pack, took out my bag and paused. I reached into my pocket for the phone and dialed, tapping each button slowly and deliberately. The phone kept ringing and with each rattle that passed I wondered if I had the right number.

Autumn had been lazy in coming. The grass stayed green longer than usual and there was grumbling among the old timers. The long suffocating afternoons of summer dragged on well into October. Any deviation from the routine was met with speculation, worry, uncertainty. What would the winter bring?

Whatever it was I was sure I could handle a few months of howling wind and snow. After all, I had grown up here, I was toughened on this weather, on this corner of forgotten land. I got through it as a newborn and later as a little boy sledding down mounds of ice and snow from morning until night. I crossed my arms and I waited. There was wood stacked in the corner of the shed, already dry, there was kindling in a basket in the kitchen. I would wait it out from behind the frosted windows, flame licking the insides of the stove, a kettle on top coming to boil, the radio playing Brahms.

Even an educated man falls prey to romantic notions. Maybe more so than others. It wasn't hard recreating from memory what life had been like back then. But there's more to it than patching together scenes of carrying wood in from the outside, light snow on the shoulders, bending over to light the fire, rubbing hands together for a job well done. When winter came it came with a fury, cold brutal nights, logs that became damp and wouldn't catch, black acrid smoke filling the inside of the house, windows open, more of the cold air coming in, the whine of the dogs, the smell of the dogs, the four of us lost in our instincts inside these four walls.

Snowed in. The literal meaning of it. No way out. The snow covering the front door, the windows, flirting with the roof. Every house only a roof decorating blankness. A few branches sticking out and pointing to the trees sleeping below.

Traveling to see her was out of the question. But that was where my first thoughts flew, not at how I was going to get out, how the dogs would get out, how I would get the wood out of the shed, dry it, start the fire, how the next few days would play out against the backdrop of this isolation.

How would I see her – that was the thought that crossed my mind when I looked out the window at first light.

I didn't know what I would say to her or even if there was anything to say. She hardly said much in return. I came here to make my peace – with what? With a past I didn't live through? With who I became in spite of myself? Something told me she might have the answer. That they all had the answer and just weren't telling me. And she, with her silence, with her enigmatic words that sounded like secrets unveiled by the wind, she seemed to know more than the others.

I thought you might need this. The words emptied of any emotion. Her scarf visibly bright against her dark coat and the white of snow. She did not have a hat on, no gloves, but in her hand a bag that had seen better days. I opened the gate and welcomed her in, the first time she had come this close to where I lived. I had to keep the dogs from putting their muddy paws on her but she didn't seem to mind. She wanted to know their names. She put the bag on the floor and tucked her hands in her coat pockets, breathing out a long sigh and looking around. It had taken me two days to dig out from under the snow. We stood now in what looked like a tunnel, its edges eye level, that wound from the front door to the front gate and to the shed where I kept the supplies. I asked her what was in the bag. Leftovers. She said if I didn't like them maybe the dogs would. It made sense. It was that simple.

The Photographer

He'd stopped photographing landscapes almost as soon as he had begun. In recent years he had stopped photographing anyone. We would walk around the city for hours, his camera swinging from its noose by his side. It was always at the ready but he would never lift it to his eyes and tell you to hold still.

"An artist has a single job, to bring something to life. But how do you give life to something that hasn't died yet?"

He used to say such things when we first met. Part of what attracted me to him I guess, the mind of an eccentric that could still tie his shoelaces and match his socks.

"I don't think most people think of it quite so literally," I remember saying once.

"Is there any other way?" It was his only reply.

Slowly the walls of his studio became bare. He either sold most of his work or gave away what he couldn't. He stopped spending time in his darkroom. Instead he paged through newspapers looking for garage sales, yard sales, estate sales, anyone moving out of town. He circled them in black then made a list with addresses and phone numbers arranged by upcoming dates.

That's how he spent most of his weekends, going from one sale to another, sometimes stopping at an antique store if there was one along the way. He had a single question when he got there: Do you have any old photographs?

Anything would do but he preferred those people looking to unload entire shoeboxes of memories. Something a distant aunt or recently deceased grandmother kept away in a dusty attic, under the bed, or in a corner of a wardrobe. If they had any he would buy the entire box.

At home he would spend hours poring over them, making piles. The children in one pile and the adults in another pile. As soon as a batch was sorted this way he would summarily toss the pile with the adults in the garbage. Hundreds of images. From one dark corner to another.

The rest of the photographs he scrutinized more closely. He would turn them over and read their inscriptions: names, places, salutations, dates. It didn't matter so much when and where the pictures were taken or who they were. He wanted to know when the photographs stopped being taken. *William ,* __________ *1923-1929.* Or anything with the words *In Loving Memory.*

Those photographs, maybe one or two out of a hundred, he held on to. And when we would go on our walks around the city he would bring along his camera and those photographs.

"Think about it," he'd say. "What's one thing you wish you did when you were little that you never got to do?"

"Oh, I don't know, I can't remember."

"C'mon, c'mon," he'd press. "There has to be something you really wanted to do but never had the chance."

"The Empire State Building I guess. I've lived my whole life in this city and I still have never been to the top of the Empire State Building. Can you believe that?"

And without a second thought he would turn and head in the direction of whatever place or thing went through my head that day. Other times he would follow his own whims and not speak a word until we got to the place that had materialized in his head. Once there he would take out his set of old photographs and flip through them, selecting the one he felt most appropriate. He would prop it up against a railing, the skyline opening up beyond, or the lights of a rollercoaster causing multicolored streaks against the darkness. Sometimes the picture lay simply in a field in Central Park, on a bench, on a seat in an old movie theater, the film rolling through the starry dust above our heads.

When the image was lined up just right he would snap a shot and pick up the old photograph and put it away at the back of the pile. And in each of the photographs, as he was looking through the viewfinder and I was looking at him looking at them, the eyes and faces of those children would stare back at us from among blades of grass or leaning on a park swing on a summer afternoon.

"Well, what did you think of the Empire State Building?" he would ask. "Billy here looked like he had a good time, don't you think?" and he would pat his side pocket with the photographs.

It started at this place called *Chez Pedro's*. But truthfully it probably started much earlier than that. Maybe it started when we were still trying to pretend to our girlfriends that we read Playboy for the articles. There were signs, but signs never come with labels that tell you that's what they are. You always figure it out when it's much too late. And on that night we were all together at the same time in the same place, seeing the same things unfold in front of our eyes, so what happened naturally had the feel of something more than it really was. At least that's how I see it in retrospect.

It was a Saturday, and it would be Frankie's last night walking as a free man among us brave holdouts, as Steve would remind us often throughout the evening. After that night, it would be all over. The noose, the ball and chain, we heard all of the clichés, especially as Steve kept pushing down whatever the bartender happened to shove in his direction.

"Goddamn, Frankie," he'd start most of his sentences.

We all referred to Frank as Frankie, which was not out of lack of respect, but because he was the youngest of the three of us. No one else had come. We'd been spread too far across the country by various turns of fate.

"You of all people," Steve seemed incredulous. "Goddamn. I can't believe you're tying the ol' knot."

Steve had always been the clown in the group. Every group's got one. But I never knew if it was all a game for him, a face he put on simply to get attention, or if that's just the way he was. Just a big kid. A big kid with a small beer belly and a five o'clock shadow.

That night we all drove to *Chez Pedro's* in my car after having dinner at Frankie's favorite grease joint. I was glad we did that. None of that fancy dinner bullshit. He'd have plenty of time for that with his soon-to-be wife. It was a bachelor party after all, or a bachelor drink fest to be more exact, not a baby shower. We ended up at *Pedro's* because we needed something to do before hitting the bars, and those would still be pretty dead for another hour or so. By Steve's meticulous calculations, it was plenty of time to get Frankie fucked up before unleashing him into his last night as a free man. Frankie's words, of course. *Pedro's* served up some mean drinks at the bar after dinner hour, so we all agreed that it was a good starting point. We could have gone to a good strip joint, but we wanted to play with the real thing.

"Don't get me wrong, Frankie. Melissa's a hell of a

great girl. She's damn hot." Frankie knew Steve didn't mean anything by that. "It's just that, damn, I mean, look around you."

Frankie looked around him at the bar. The scene was disappointing.

"Ok, Ok. Bad example," Steve backtracked. "I'm only saying that the options are limitless. Well, not really limitless, but pretty damn close, you know what I mean? And you're just going to shut the door in the face of opportunity. With two words. Bang! Done."

We didn't ask exactly what opportunity it was that Steve was referring to. I'm not sure it would have mattered. He said things like that. It's what Steve did, and we all knew it was never too long until he turned philosophical on us on any given night. He was our beer bottle prophet, and we could always depend on his cryptic words of wisdom to add a bit of color to a dull scene.

"You need to get off my case. I'm getting married and I'm happy about it. You just wish you'd done everything I did. I've had my share of fun. When you were sitting in your room jerking off because Beth left your dumb ass, I was out getting laid," Frankie protested, with what Steve detected was a bit too much coherence for a man who should have been getting wasted. We were doing too much talking, too little drinking, he remarked astutely.

Frankie had a good point, though. Girls tended to stay away from Steve as best as they could when they found out that he didn't have an *Off* button. He was the same full-steam-ahead Steve at all times, whether it was over lunch, coffee, at bars or parties, seven days a week, day and night. Steve was a great guy, but it took some time to get used to him, and no one had gotten used to him for longer than we had. We loved him like a brother. He just wasn't the relationship type. Which is exactly the reason why he thought he was the perfect guy to give relationship advice to anyone who'd managed to keep a girlfriend for longer than two weeks.

Steve's reasoning went something like this: It's like when you're playing a really intense game of Super Mario Brothers, the original, pixels and all, and you've been playing for hours and your thumb's getting numb and your eyes are having trouble focusing, but you finally get to the end of the level. Your adrenaline is pumping, and you're face to face with *The Boss*, and you freak out because you don't know what's going to come out of his mouth, and the next thing you know you're dead. Not because you're a bad player, but you just didn't see it coming because you were too focused on staying alive. Now, if you had someone there with you watching from the sidelines, say, Steve (he always volunteered himself as an example), he'd be able to observe what was happening from a different perspective and give you pointers on how to better approach the situation next time. It really made complete sense if you played as much Super Mario Brothers as we did growing up. Otherwise, it probably just sounds asinine coming out of the mouth of a thirty-year-old.

We had spent about as long as we could at *Pedro's* drinking by ourselves before I pointed out how pathetic we must have looked and suggested moving on to someplace with a significant female contingent so that at least it would appear as if we were being pathetic for a reason.

By then it was after eleven, and it wasn't too difficult to find a bar with what we were looking for, which was single women, but not necessarily so. We weren't picky that night. Steve just wanted to be the guy who gave Frankie his last memorable night before getting married. He took pride in that.

We entered the first place that was loud and looked like it had attracted enough people to make it interesting. The more bodies the better. It was *The Tavern On...* something or other street. Steve decreed that it was perfect, which means it must have been. He had an eye for these things.

"All right. Now that's what I'm talking about, see?" he said as we walked in, and waved his outstretched arm with palm facing up in a big arc across the room as if he was a guide showing us yet undiscovered territory. "The land of opportunity."

We had taken too long between drinks so we were all unnecessarily sober, even by my count. We went up to the bar and ordered a double round of shots that we downed in quick succession. After the shots, we each fisted a beer and turned from the bar to the center of the room to survey what we had to work with.

"Frankie!" Steve said loudly as if he was across the room. "Now we need to get you to have some fun."

That's exactly what Frankie was worried about. He and Steve had very different definitions of what fun was, but this was his bachelor party. He had to go along with it because that was part of the rules. We were all that was left. But somewhere in the back of his mind there was still the promise he'd made to Melissa that he wouldn't do anything stupid or crazy. He'd promised because he loved her, and because she trusted him, and he didn't want to lose that trust.

Steve, of course, easily dismissed Frankie's concerns and pleas to take it easy before we'd headed out for the evening with his usual logic.

"Crazy is a relative term, Frankie. Let me explain," he'd said to him. "As long as everyone's alive by morning then no harm done. Any questions?"

We weren't at the bar for too long when Steve walked up to the first group of girls that his eyes fell on. The minute you stop looking is the minute you stop living, was his motto. Once he'd reached the group, he selected one of them and whispered something in her ear. The girl walked back with Steve, a big grin on his face. He bought the girl a bottle of beer and handed it to her. She stood in front of Frankie, almost nose to nose, and proceeded to lick the neck of the bottle slowly, looking at him the whole time.

Then she put the entire neck of the bottle in her mouth and moved it up and down. When she was done she gave Frankie a kiss on the cheek, smiled and squeaked "Congratulations!" then walked away back to her friends.

"Told you it'd be a good place," Steve said, proud of himself.

Frankie was not exactly complaining, either. He began to loosen up.

"Ok. Now it's your turn. We'll start slow," Steve instructed. "Find any girl you like and go up to her. You gotta get her to kiss you anywhere but on your cheek or forehead."

"I thought we were starting slow?" Frankie protested.

"We are. This is slow. Don't be a pussy," Steve snapped back, with exactly the kind of playground logic that you can't argue with because any argument becomes automatically self-incriminating unless you can prove it otherwise. It's the mature and grown-up version of, "What? Are you chicken?" Arguing with it only proves that your accuser is correct, so you might as well not even try, leaving you with the only viable option, and that is proving him wrong.

Frankie performed his task by approaching a blonde that Steve had labeled behind his back as "a solid 5." He got her to lick his right earlobe. "You sort of cheated," I told him when he got back to the bar, just to give him a hard time. He shrugged his shoulders, feigning innocence.

We spent the next hour or so putting Frankie through more stupid and childish missions. We made him convince a girl to let him suck her toes, which was just plain cruel. It all got easier for him to perform as the night wore on and inhibitions went out the window.

Frankie's last task was to find a girl who would be willing to take off her bra so he could wear it on his head. By then everyone in the bar knew what we were up to, and even some of the girls were egging him on. It wouldn't be hard to find a willing contributor. Frankie made his way toward a tall redhead, a girl he knew he would have never had a chance with if they were both sober. He'd finally figured out the point of the game. She had been looking in his direction throughout the night and had smirked a few times as they made eye contact.

I finally had to tell him, "Frankie, just do it already. You know you want to, so just get it over with." We were having fun.

I could tell he liked the girl because he didn't just go up to her and ask. He started a whole conversation with her, probably told her his real name (never a good idea in these situations), where he worked, where he lived, typical flirting bullshit.

Steve and I were sitting on our stools at the bar waiting for him to make a move, and he just kept standing there chatting, smiling, laughing. When she bit her lip I knew it wouldn't end that easily. We'd put so much alcohol in Frankie that he probably didn't even remember he was getting married in less than a month and thought that he was still on the market.

Frankie and the redhead talked some more, speaking into each other's ear to compensate for the loud music. Then the girl grabbed his hand and walked with him weaving toward the women's bathroom. They disappeared inside. Finally he was going to get her to take something off.

We waited for him to come back out triumphant. We waited much longer than it takes to remove a bra, and we even took into consideration the probable loss of hand-eye coordination but reasoned that the minimal amount of clothing his new friend had been wearing would make up for that. It was a simple mathematical equation.

Frankie came out of the bathroom alone after what seemed like an eternity with none of the spoils of victory we had expected.

"What the fuck, Frankie?" Steve began to give him a hard time. "You had that one in the bag, man. What more does a girl need to do? You didn't…?"

"No. We didn't. Just shut up for a minute," Frankie looked confused, but it wasn't the alcohol. He was actually trying to think about something and was searching for a way to put it into words.

"Shit, man. You did!" Steve persisted.

"No, I fuckin' didn't, Ok? It's not like that," Frankie was getting visibly agitated now.

"Then what the hell's your problem? Was she a dude?" Steve plowed ahead without the *Off* button.

"She took pictures, alright. She had this camera and she

just whipped it out and started taking pictures of the two of us. What was I supposed to do? She was half naked."

"Shit! That's all? So what's the problem?" Steve laughed, and Frankie shot him a look that told him it wasn't a joke.

"The problem is that now there's these pictures of me and this naked chick and who knows where the fuck they're going to end up. This could ruin my career, not to mention that Melissa would kill me. She'd call the whole thing off."

"Alright. Relax, Frankie. It's gonna be fine," I said, just trying to keep him from panicking. In fact, I didn't know if it would be all right or not. It's just what friends usually say in those situations for lack of something better.

By then we were all sobering up. Something like that will kill a buzz faster than dunking your head in cold water. The redhead had also come back out of the bathroom and was the center of conversation among the group of friends she had come with. Frankie was sure she was showing them the pictures.

"I need to get those pictures. We can't leave like this," Frankie had begun to panic despite my feeble attempt to prevent it.

Steve had been silent for some time, which worried me.

"This is what I need you to do, Frankie," he said, snapping out of his trance like a soldier taking control of his unit in a time of crisis.

He called the three of us together in a huddle and whispered his plan so he wouldn't have to yell it over the music. When he was done Frankie looked at him without saying anything for a few seconds.

"I can't believe I'm doing this. I can't fuckin' believe this," Frankie shook his head, and got up from his stool.

He walked straight to the redhead and began talking her up again. She was a bit taller than him, so she had to lower her head when he wanted to tell her something. She smiled. It was a good sign. He had to go slow for Steve's plan to work, so we didn't mind waiting. I even went up to one of her friends and struck up a conversation so that they wouldn't be interrupted as much.

Eventually Frankie and the girl disappeared again, this time in the men's room. Steve followed them in while I waited outside.

Steve came back out first this time with a satisfied grin on his face. I said goodbye to the redhead's friend and sat back down at the bar with Steve.

"Done," he said.

"Good. He was really freaking out. I felt bad," I replied.

The girl came out and Frankie followed her a few seconds later. When he arrived at the bar I noticed he was shaking.

"You have nothing to worry about, kid," Steve beamed at him, patting his jeans pocket. "Call it a night?"

We were all more than glad to leave the place and get Frankie back to his house. In the car he was completely quiet.

"What's the problem? I got the card. She doesn't even

know the difference. Her bag was on the floor and she was clearly preoccupied. You don't have to worry about shit Frankie, all right? It's over," Steve said from the backseat over Frankie's shoulder, who was sitting in the front just staring at the road.

"It's not over," he said quietly.

"All right. Ok, look," Steve had that tone in his voice again. "Remember your first car? What was it? A piece of shit Dodge, right? I remember that car. It was great, for a POS. We had some great times with that car, didn't we? I know you loved it because you washed it and polished it every weekend even though it was starting to get rust holes in the frame. But no matter how much you loved that car, you had to let it go, right?"

"I'm not leaving Melissa because of this, asshole! She's not a goddamn Dodge," Frankie snapped.

"Listen. Just let me finish. That's not what I'm saying," Steve was determined to finish. "It was a great little beater, but remember how much fun it was going to look for a new car? The new paint? The new car smell?"

"I did more than just look tonight, Steve," Frankie said with regret in his voice.

"Ok. So it was more like a test drive," Steve laughed.

"You're a moron, you know that? They're not fuckin' cars, you realize that? There's a reason no woman will come near you," Frankie was just mad now.

"That's not cool, Frankie. Steve just saved your ass," I

said, trying to defuse the situation.

"He didn't save shit. If it wasn't for him it never would've happened in the first place," Frankie's voice was getting louder and angrier.

"Frankie, no one forced you to do anything you didn't want to do tonight," I said. "That last bit? Sometimes we just need to make choices."

As soon as I'd said it, I regretted that I did. There was no point in giving him an even bigger guilt trip, and we were as much to blame as he was. Frankie was already beating himself up enough on his own.

In the back seat Steve had barely noticed our exchange.

"And even better, no one's ever gonna know. No harm, no foul," Steve said matter-of-factly.

"I'm gonna know, Steve," Frankie said.

"Yea. You'll always have the mental pictures. Or you can just print these out," Steve chuckled, throwing the memory card on Frankie's lap.

He then proceeded to say something about headlights and a cloth top, to which Frankie turned around and punched him on the shoulder.

"Heh heh. You're just pissed off 'cause you know I'm right," Steve said while rubbing his shoulder.

"You're a bastard. You really are," were Frankie's last words to us for the rest of the ride.

When he got out of the car none of us said goodbye. Steve and I drove off in silence for some time.

"Well, at least he'll remember this one," Steve said, proud of himself, then got settled more comfortably in the passenger seat. He looked ahead like an artist reflecting on the distance.

Counting The Rain

There is a gust of wind. Short, but powerful, unmistakable. Then, two seconds later, another burst, longer and mournful. They alternate. The shorts gusts and the longer ones, two seconds apart.

There are twelve steps from the street to the front door of Michael's office. The office is in a turn-of-the-century building on Delancey, a dark, narrow street, more of a lane if you ask me, just off the boulevard. I liked it for its dirty quaintness, its been-there-forever trees cracking the sidewalk. Most people would say that there are thirteen steps from the street to the front door of Michael's office but that's not exactly true. If you stand on the sidewalk and begin counting, not there, not where you stand, but with the first step you land on, then there are twelve steps. I know what they say, but you do not count the landing, the area where your ascent ends and you are face to face with the door. Let me explain. We've already established that when you stand on the sidewalk you do not count the sidewalk as a first step. Now let's imagine you have just come out of Michael's office, or any office for that matter, and you are standing on the landing, about to descend. Naturally you would not consider that as step number one. You would begin counting with the first step that follows and continue on down until you get to twelve, once again omitting the sidewalk from your calculations. Why? It only stands to reason that if one does not count a step upon ascending the stairs, one also does not consider it upon descending. So what most people would count as a first and last step doesn't really count! Yes, I know what it sounds like, but that's just it, that's the problem. Most people don't bother with these things. They go around all day believing that there are thirteen stairs instead of twelve and never think anything of it. These people go around half the day half wrong most of the time.

Michael's office was lined with wooden shelves from wall to wall. There was hardly any blank space in there. The shelves were full of books, mostly manuals from what I could tell, the kind where the spines look identical and are labeled in either gold or silver letters. What is not covered by books is covered by tapes. I would say there were an equal amount of books and tapes but I didn't want to upset him so I didn't take the chance to count them all. I don't want to tell you something that might be inaccurate.

Between the gusts of wind there are also other sounds. Something like the rustle of branches and the scratch of leaves against pavement. These come in between the wind sounds but not every time. Sometimes there is only a pause that follows the first gust, a whiteness, silence; one imagines snow falling. Then the gusts resume, tearing the air outside. At first that little aberration threw off my timing, but I got it eventually. Not a simple algorithm but that's what I enjoyed most about it.

The first time I went to see Michael I decided to walk although it was late January and a bitter cold had set in after what had been a mostly mild December. The streets were coated for the first time in a light snow and I liked that because it made everything seem to slow down, to take a deep breath and consider the next possible move. Imagine the house in front of you, snug in its frame, pausing just for a moment, a fraction of second, then going on about its business of creaking and swaying, of whatever else it is that houses do. It was that kind of day.

That was also the day I noticed that there were twelve steps leading up to Michael's door. In fact, every house along Delancey had twelve steps leading from the sidewalk to the front door. Some had black metal railings and some not, but unmistakably each one had twelve steps. I didn't tell Michael this, of course. He would be the first one to know, likely having counted those same stairs hundreds, if not thousands of times going in and out of that front door.

Rain is tricky. It takes days to get used to it. At first there is nothing familiar about it. Each drop seems to come of its own accord whenever it wishes, striking the house (or window? hard to tell sometimes) with either a flat or sharp sound depending, I presume, on whether the roof is made of slate, tin, or cheap tile. When there is no house, when it's just you and the forest, for example, you have to tune in to the way it strikes a leaf or the trunk of a tree or a rock. But even that's not impossible. It can be done. It just takes a little longer. As in any melody there must be a mark, or several, which indicates a shift, a sign for the bassoonist or the violinist to take up another note and carry it for the indicated measure. If you keep track of these movements you will notice that sooner or later they correspond, there is some symmetry built into what to the untrained ear sounds like chaos.

You see, that's what Michael understood. That's why he and I had such a great connection. We didn't need to talk about these things. Those obvious, trivial things that only imbeciles would dwell on. I could go on about anything else I pleased and he knew what I meant. One day I threw a horrible fit at the dry cleaner when I asked them please not to write my name in permanent ink upon each garment. I know who I am, for God's sake! I know my own name! Well, after too much time had been wasted they apologized, something or other about company policy, that it's for the customer's benefit, etc. etc. Needless to say I will not be taking my clothes there again. Michael listened to that story with what I could only describe as restrained amusement and nodded a few times during the course of the narrative. He knew! He just knew!

If I had a favorite sound I would say the ocean crashing on the shore. Or against a jetty. They're both wonderful sounds. Most people would confuse the two, consider them interchangeable, but it's clear that one is more soothing, a honeyed sound, whereas the other is cacophonous, more violent. Two lazy waves rolling onto the shores, then the more thunderous breaking of water against rock. How beautifully the two go together. The first sound makes each second drag, interminable almost, then the next one grabs it by the throat and slams it to the ground. Oh, I could tell you how this battle plays out to the very last minute.

Michael would let me borrow anything I wanted from his shelves. At first I took books but I just couldn't see what he saw in them. I would lie in bed reading and every few pages or so I would have to stop and let my mind wander. It went on like that for hours until finally I would put the book down, fold my arms across my chest and remain in that position until morning.

When I brought the books back he just placed them on the shelf and didn't say anything. He would simply ask me if I wanted another. I think the first few times I said yes because I wanted to please him. I didn't want him to think I was being ungrateful. I would take another book, place it on the table next to me, saying I would read it when I had time but I knew that I wouldn't get through it. But if I told him I would read it then I knew we would understand each other. One time he was so eager to hear what had happened earlier that day that I knew it would be no use telling him I did not sleep a wink with his last offering. I think it was summer then. Again I had walked to his place, this time leaving a half hour earlier than usual. I wanted to give myself time to go through the park. The benches were freshly painted and the smell of paint still lingered in their vicinity. I found them to be ugly. I never really thought about it before but there was something hideous about those benches that day. I didn't realize what it was until I began telling Michael about my walk, he with his gentle nature listening with a curiosity I felt made it my responsibility to fulfill. Until that day I didn't realize what bothered me. I had crossed through that park so many times that I knew exactly how many benches there were and exactly how many paces between each one (if one walked with a slow, measured gait, something of a lazy stroll, not quite a full walk). I even knew how many horizontal slats made up the seats and the backs (the exact number being irrelevant to the point of the story). I knew all of these details so well that I stopped paying attention, I stopped counting. Can you imagine that? The moment you know something so incredibly well it no longer exists as itself in all its complexity, in the minute details that give it a distinguished life of its own.

Michael knew all of this. I could tell because he seemed

to become annoyed more than usual that day. How long has it been since you slept? That's all that Michael said when I told him. I don't know, I said. Actually I knew exactly how many days it had been, but I didn't want to upset him.

If you asked me if I had a favorite sound it would have to be that of thunder. Not just rain, but an all out thunderstorm when the sky feels as if it's cracking above your head, the rumble lasting inside the echo, inside your chest still beating from being caught off guard. I take special delight in that. Being surprised once in a while. Imagining the whole house shaking from the aftershock. That one kept me up for days. Especially since there is no lightning to go by. If you had lightning then you could at least predict that thunder could possibly follow. Though of course even then it's not certain, but at least it is probable. Without it what do you have to go by? Silence. All you have is silence. And have you ever tried to measure silence? I don't mean just counting out a few minutes at a time in your head. Children can play that game. I mean night after night staying up and keeping a running count in your head between each thunderclap. Knowing that the only thing that matters is the silence or it all falls apart. Sometimes it is all that prisoners have to keep from going crazy in solitary. They're in there all alone with only their own thoughts for company. That and the silence between scheduled interruptions. You see, this is no different.

The last time I stopped by to see Michael we sat down

and were about to launch into our usual chat (I was holding a cup of tea and one of the lemon cookies he always
keeps around) when he asked, How long has it been since
you slept? I said I don't know, last night I was playing…
He interrupted, asking me, Steven, how long does it take
for the sea to roll onto the beach six times? Thirty seconds,
I said. Of course he knew that, so I didn't know why he
asked in the first place. Then he asked, How many times
does the wind howl in one minute? That one was easy, thirteen times. Michael leaned back in his chair and remained
silent for a while. He does that a lot. His eyes seemed to
search the walls of his office, the ones full of books and
tapes, which by now I'd listened to hundreds of times. This
time he didn't get up and pick another from its place and
say, Let's give this a try.

When I walked out of the office I counted all of the
twelve steps it took me to get to the sidewalk. I counted
exactly forty-nice paces to the crosswalk at the end of the
block. Did you know there are five stoplights between Michael's and your place? Isn't it peculiar that the first flight
leading to your door has six steps but the second flight has
seven? I would have taken the elevator but it seems rather
slow, at least four seconds from one floor to the next.

From a Few Tables Away

You sit a few tables away, watching a man struggle to take off the cap from a small bottle of wine. You judge that he is old, but not that old. Maybe the bottle then, maybe there is something wrong with the bottle, some flaw in manufacturing. He twists the cap left and right to loosen it, he taps the bottom of the bottle, he shakes it until the liquid forms a pinkish foam. Yes, definitely the bottle you conclude.

He's been at it for some time. When he grows tired, exhausted and frustrated with his efforts, he pauses briefly, turns the bottle over in his hand, holds it up to the light, scrutinizes the label, maybe for a secret answer, some coded instructions he might have overlooked previously. Nothing.

You consider offering to help. At least that's the thought that goes through your head as you watch him struggle. It is a natural thought. No more than that. Are you feeling a bit guilty just now for that twinge of pleasure you sensed while watching him? Ah, never mind, it is his struggle you tell yourself. None of your business. He could quit at any time. One must know what the stakes are before engaging in any lengthy endeavor. But doesn't he in some odd way seem to enjoy his frustration? You're almost sure of it. See the corner of his mouth lift just a little?

Nonetheless, you do consider offering to help. At the very least you consider the option. It would only be appropriate. In the end no one likes to be thought of as a bad person, one who takes pleasure in the misery of others. How could you allow yourself to give off such an impression, even if only to yourself, by ignoring this man's struggle? You look on as the man pauses and takes up the bottle again, twists at its neck in vain. Of course, the desire to help him is now stronger than ever.

You think about it some more and choose to do nothing. But not without reason, with the best of intentions. Would that man not feel the worse for it if you offered to help? Just imagine how he might feel if you should come along and say, "Let me try." Imagine the impertinence of that simple phrase. I know you have, that's why you're still watching him work away at the bottle, satisfied with your distance. You've pictured the blankness that would certainly fall over the man's face as he stares at the impossible choice laid out before him as clear as daylight: one, if he should agree to let you try your luck at the stubborn bottle, he would be admitting to himself and to another man that he is not capable enough to do the necessary work himself; two, if he should decline, however politely, he would still be faced with the unopened bottle, the wine either an eternal prisoner of poor design or of his own incompetence. Surely he would be left in a state of complete misery, you as its cause.

So you keep watching from a few tables away and think to yourself, *If only someone would help this man. If only someone would.* You grieve for the corner you're in, you wish for him dearly this minor victory. How happy he would be to say, finally, "I did it". And he would think then that his happiness was wholly his – though you would be happy too, maybe a bit proud, knowing how difficult the decision had been.

The Sea

The air is musty and there is an old woman in the center, her head covered in black cloth tied under her chin. I know there is a woman in the room even though I can't see her face. I see something silver, it's a liquid, then soon after something that looks like an X. There are other people in the room, familiar, but I can't see them either. They're looking on and they seem worried.

I've told my mother that story several times over the years whenever the broken images shifted through my head. I would ask if she knew what they meant. Instead of answering the question, she would tell me about the nightmares. Those I remember more clearly.

I am walking along the coast on a day with no sun. The forecast predicted rain, so there isn't much time. I pace the beach, empty of people, needing none, while blue-gray clouds slide overhead like a coffin lid.

In the nightmares, the sky glazes over, one big pane of glass collecting dust from the edges inward. I stand in the middle of somewhere waiting for light to flee from the advance of a convergent rim of clouds. When the light is gone, darkness shines like hardened tar and I can see my reflection in front of me.

The two of us stand face to face in the vacant heart of no day, no night, neither of us wanting to make the first move. I keep my eyes open to make sure he doesn't.

While the sky darkens, the sea pulls a layer of mist around its wide shoulders like a feathered blanket. Something about it even feels warm, welcoming. At that moment I could even imagine being part of, understanding something of that size.

Each night my parents would find me standing in front of a tall mirror in our apartment, staring ahead, utterly still. I didn't respond when they called my name. I couldn't hear. My mother cried. They tried to shake me awake. They said it was as if I had died standing up. My father had to pick me up in his arms to carry me back to bed. I felt so heavy, they said, that it took all of his strength to tear me away from the mirror.

A wave gushes over the beach and covers the shore as far to the left and right as the eye could reach. The crease in the sea smoothes itself out and gathers back into the fold, leaving behind burdens, secrets, stories about dreams.

When it began happening regularly they tried putting me to sleep in different places, but I always found a mirror in the night. I would stop in front of it and open my eyes, staring into the darkest distance.

It wasn't normal, my mother said. So she took me to doctors, specialists, there were tests, nothing conclusive, not much to worry about. Which, for her, meant there was everything to worry about. So she did the only thing left that could be done. But she never told me. My aunt blurted it out one day, casually, as if it were the simplest of things.

Retreating, the sea trickles between bare toes and trails of broken shells. It whispers and hisses that it could always come back for more, thirsty and willing. It could wash up on the same shore and take me back too, sliding with the undertow. I cannot stop listening and I cannot turn from the crashing waves, eyes forward, watching as it swallows everything under.

"What you remember is a gypsy doing white magic. Your grandmother knew her. What she poured on the ground formed the shape of a cross. That's the X you saw in your sleep. After that you stopped having nightmares."

After that I stopped remembering my dreams. I wake up with no memory of the hours that passed during the night. I wake up not knowing if I dream at all.

I want to ask about that, if it was all part of the bargain, if the answer always carries such a heavy price. And I want to ask what the sea knew about all of this. Will it tell me again if I listen long enough, if I stand firm at its feet and look it dead in the eye?

Sneak Attack

This place could take a first timer and grind him down into a figment of what he was when he arrived. It was racing season, high summer, the Hotel Adeline. Old world charm and a quaint "Hello…" "Have a wonderful…" "How was your…" and, "It sure is a lovely afternoon…" Like so many bygones tucked away along the interstate.

There was a cigar store down one of the side streets, still owned by an old, thin Italian, a throwback to a time when stores didn't need more than a hand-painted sign swinging in the breeze. The wood was worn and the windows clouded with age. I knew about it from a guy who knew a guy who heard from someone else. All part of the charm.

I'd been friends with Elizabeth longer than anyone I could still call a friend. Out of college, young, eager, good at what we did. One of the worst times of my life. But I had fond memories of those days, when nothing more ever happened than getting from A to B. In that sense they were simpler. We had a few brief romantic moments then, never anything serious. She knew me, and because of that I felt I owed her something, but wasn't sure what. Agreeing to dinner was the best I could come up with.

"You look great," Elizabeth said, doing the cheek to cheek outside the restaurant.

"You too."

"I really need this. We all do. Isn't it a wonderful place?" she asked, my answer unnecessary.

I knew she needed to exorcise some demons in the silence I could give her, which is all I really had to give.

"Right," she said, and we moved on past the awkward stage. We pretended we were there for the meal and that it did not reek too much of the intervention that it really was.

Small talk about work, people we knew, the market, etc. Much said about not much at all. In a way it felt like we had picked up where we left off years ago. But it wouldn't end there. I knew that. Conversations like these never did. It was a bad appetizer before the main course. You'd already heard what the special was and you knew you wouldn't like it but were forced to order it anyway because the person you were with said that it was just to die for, not to miss, and so on and so forth and so you sat there waiting, just waiting slowly for it to arrive.

"The last few months have been disastrous. The divorce did me in. The son of a bitch was ruthless. He fought me for every little thing."

There it was. It had come to that. I sat there playing the receptacle we call a good friend, responsible for the well-timed nod. We have no way out of this. There is no advice that can rise above our own transgressions. That's what shrinks are for, and even they do a poor job of it most of the time.

"Of course we both knew it was inevitable," Elizabeth said. "It was going to end one way or another. It was just a matter of how long we could stick it out. For the kids at least."

It was always the same. Money or sex got in the way and the kids were caught in the crossfire. Most of us know more middle-aged people looking for a second chance at romance that any one of us could start a match-making service, if there weren't already hundreds out there suggesting how to fix a life.

When you have nothing to offer, I've learned you can at least offer your time. I asked Elizabeth if she wanted to come to the track.

A familiar voice called out over the noise like a bullhorn. We spotted him and he waved us over.

"First race of the season, big guy? Just got here? How's it feel? *Sneak Attack*, I'm tellin' ya, *Sneak Attack*, just a hunch," he winked and made a clicking sound with the corner of his mouth. He had it all figured out. Everyone here has it all figured out – the wines, the dinners, the races, the weather, the charm of it, all of the goddamn charm you could stomach.

"Who's this?" he continued without pausing. Stan was the kind of person who never needed anyone else to have a conversation.

"Oh, sorry. This is Elizabeth. Old friend, known each other since right out of college."

They shook hands and Elizabeth excused herself for a minute and disappeared into the noise.

"Not bad, not bad at all," he said, nodding and slapping my shoulder.

"Oh, it's nothing," I tried to explain. Why did it feel like an argument? Like I needed to defend myself in front of him? "Lots of history, you know. Plus she's just getting over a really bad divorce."

"So? I'm tellin' ya, not bad at all," he concluded, *finis*. How do you argue with *that*?

Sneak Attack won, which I knew would happen. When the horse crossed the finish line I turned a wry smile and hated the whole place for it, hated the whole goddamn town.

Inside the taxi back to The Adeline I watched the salmon sky disappear behind rooftops. It sunk with agonizing slowness. Before going in I lit a cigar and like a fish sucked the first few drags into my mouth, letting the smoke drift into the open. In the stillness of the evening light I must have looked like the silhouette of a statue of myself, the air surrounding me unnaturally cold.

"Damn fine night, isn't it?"

A voice passing in the dark. I agreed that it was.

For the first time I left the Adeline before my stay was up. I got in the car and drove. Just kept on driving away from it all. I tried to take in every twist of the road, every rotting barn hanging on by the roadside where it'd been dying slowly for years. I drove until I couldn't recognize anything anymore, and it was quiet in the car and peaceful, as if there was someone right there beside me.

The Missing Button

His apartment was filled with coffee cans and those coffee cans were filled with buttons. It wasn't really a collection; more like storage space. It had taken him years to gather all of them.

Whatever you do, don't call him a criminal. He doesn't agree with the term. A crime is something like stealing wallets or purses or breaking into a home, or hot wiring a car. Stuff like that. What he did was harmless.

"How many people do you know who could sew?" he would ask.

I had to agree that I didn't know many people who could sew.

"Exactly. Now how many people do you know who could sew a button?"

Again I had to agree that I didn't know many people who could sew a button.

"Sewing a button the right way so that it holds and doesn't come off easily is art, my friend, it takes skill."

He would expound his philosophy to anyone who would listen. Sewing buttons is not the first thing people think about when you mention sewing, this is true. Most people conjure up an image of a hole in a sock that needs mending, or a stitch that has come undone. A button is rarely imagined. And yet buttons take more of a beating than most other features of one's clothing. The workhorse of the fashion industry is how he put it. That was the first thing you had to understand to understand what he did.

His job was simple, but not exactly easy. To get people to think about the button. And not just to think about it but to have to replace it, to have to handle the needle and thread and feel the roundness of this almost forgotten utility.

His tools: a straight razor and foldable travel scissors, the kind that you could find in most dollar store sewing kits. His workshop: crowded buses or subways, a busy line at the super market. It was in those places that he'd perfected the removal of buttons. Coats, bags, back pockets, you name it. If he found the opportunity he would remove the button. Once at home he would drop them into one of the many containers and he would be happy.

What did he imagine? The surprise on someone's face when they realized their overcoat made it home in the evening with one less button than when it left? The annoyance or even outright anger now that someone couldn't wear their favorite item? No, there was no pleasure in that. He wasn't a criminal after all, he wasn't a bad guy.

"For many people," he would explain, "this is the first time they've really had to consider a button and how important that round piece of plastic or bone really is. This is the first time they've really had to think about a button."

Now consider all of the events such a small thing set in motion once it was no longer there; this part is when he really lit up. To replace a button you need another button. There really is no way around that. If your coat did not come with replacement buttons you need to find a store that sells loose buttons. And you have to find the place and you have to go there and you have to root through piles of buttons to find the right one, just a single button that can do the job right and would collaborate with the rest of the buttons. There you are then, lucky to have found your button and you go home with that nearly weightless possession and a small smirk on your face that you succeeded in something.

And maybe, just maybe, he hoped, there were a few people sitting down right now at the kitchen table, needle and thread in hand, a replacement button in the other, figuring out how to sew. Picture the deliberate small movements, the precision required to line it up just right, the concentration, the time it takes to do nothing else but fix your coat while ignoring everything, all the other stuff that for a moment doesn't mean a thing.

The Man Of Many Names

Daniel didn't notice the girl next to him. He was thinking of something else entirely.

"Hello, handsome. You're not from around here, are you?" she asked, her face so close when she bent toward him that he could smell the Wintermint of her chewing gum.

"Not really."

"Quiet, too. You don't look like you're having fun. Are you having fun?"

"Yes."

"Hmm. Then why aren't you smiling?"

"I'm having fun." A small grin crossed his lips, mostly so she'd stop asking.

"It's a quiet night," she said, motioning with her chin to the empty row of chairs arranged around the stage that extended in front of them in an elevated rectangle. "Can I sit down?"

"Sure. Go ahead."

"Thanks. These shoes do a number on my feet after a

while." She sat down in the chair to his right, then to prove her point picked up her right leg and rolled the ankle, waving a four-inch black patent leather heel.

The stage was empty save for a few revolving neon lights that sliced the floor in repeating patterns. The patterns exhausted themselves and started up again every thirty seconds or so, according to Daniel's calculations, giving off the appearance of something new and fresh. The music had shifted tempo to something a bit slower and the volume had been turned down a notch. It was a sign that the next dancer was getting ready backstage and would be out shortly.

Daniel was one of only two men sitting around the stage, the other an old man probably bored but too tired to get up and go home.

"My name's Heaven," the girl said, extending her hand for a shake.

Daniel turned slightly, shook her hand then turned back to the lights cutting each other into colorful fragments that reassembled with a flicker.

"What's your name?" she asked, realizing Daniel wasn't going to volunteer the information.

"Tony," he answered, even though he could've used the name everyone knew him by at work, which was also not his name. The foreman knew him as Miguel. The other men who went to the bar together after leaving the fields also knew him as Miguel. It was the name he'd chosen this particular season. In every city he went to find work he used a different name. There were no papers that said otherwise, no one to contradict him.

"Hi, Tony. Nice to meet you. This your first time here?"

"Yes." Daniel hesitated for a moment, not sure if he should go on, but he knew names were important to most people, so he asked. "How did you get the name Heaven?"

"It wasn't always Heaven. My roommates gave this one to me. We were sitting around getting high one night after someone stole the bag with all my stuff, my clothes, money, phone, everything. I had nothing. I'd been keeping all my money in that bag, saving it up, you know, so I could make a big deposit. And then, just like that, some jerk asshole brought me right back to zero. Nada."

"That doesn't sound like Heaven at all," Daniel said, sensing she had paused in her story to allow him to say something, anything, preferably a sympathetic word.

"Damn right it don't. I was so pissed off that night that when the joint came my way I kept pulling and pulling like I didn't want to let go, just wanted to fill my lungs with that stuff, keep all of it to myself. Someone said 'Damn girl, if you got any higher, you'd be in heaven,' and everyone laughed at that, so from then on my nickname was Heaven, and I guess it just stuck."

"What's your real name?"

"Can't say that. You know the rules," Heaven said, giving Daniel a friendly poke in the arm.

"I don't know the rules."

"Safety reasons. We all have stage names. You know, just in case of stalkers. Vanilla, Champagne, Star, Mercedes, Lexus. Thank God I didn't end up with one of those car names. I think they're tacky."

Daniel didn't know what the big deal was if she'd told him her real name. People he knew had many real names. He had several, and didn't think he'd ever run out. Ever since the coyote dropped them off in the desert ten years ago and vanished, leaving them stranded to fend for themselves in the cold of night and sweltering heat of mid afternoon, Daniel knew that to survive he'd have to become someone else.

Not all of them made it out of the desert and across the border. The first name he became in America was Alejandro, the name of the dead man whose shirt he stripped to keep warm. Survival. The real Alejandro wouldn't need the shirt or the name anymore. In America, when Daniel jumped in the back of the first pickup truck along with ten other men to drive out to the fields, no one even asked for his name. Names were for those who were more than ghosts in a different shade of skin.

A dancer had come on stage and now the lights were cutting up her body, too, falling first on her skin that glowed yellow in the fickle light, then scattering onto the floor like bits of colored glass.

"You wanna sit at the bar?" Heaven asked.

"No thanks. I don't want a drink."

"I wasn't asking if you wanted a drink."

"Then what did you ask?"

"I was asking if you'd buy *me* a drink."

"Why didn't you just say that?"

Daniel wondered why people never say what they really want. He followed the lights on the dancer's body moving to keep up with the music, which had a tempo much faster than the lights, so that the whole spectacle was out of sync, making him dizzy.

"I don't know why I didn't say it. I shouldn't have to say it. How come you won't say it?"

"Say what?"

"Say what you want. You know, why you're here."

"I don't know what I want."

"Yes, you do. Otherwise you wouldn't be here. Everyone here knows *exactly* what they want. The girls want money to buy nice clothes to get that nice husband who's going to take them away from this place. The men want a wife who won't nag, a car that will start up every morning, a good blowjob they don't have to ask for. We all dream in cliches, but no one here ever says that, of course."

That's not what Daniel wanted, not tonight.

The old man slipped a dollar bill under a garter belt that cut into the dancer's thigh. Daniel left his own dollar bill on the ledge and watched the woman pick it up the way one would pick up a dirty piece of tissue paper off the floor.

Just something that needed to be done.

"All right. What would you like to drink?" Daniel said, getting up and for the first time noticing all the women that stood around behind the stage, leaning on walls, waiting, just waiting, proof that it was indeed a slow night.

At the bar he ordered a beer for himself and sat down next to the girl. Ice clinked in her glass. She stirred red straws in a red drink out of habit.

"So what do you do, Tony?" Heaven asked.

"I'm in construction," Daniel said without hesitation, a small lie, hoping the dirt under his fingernails was convincing enough. Back home he'd always wanted to make things, to build things that would last long after he was gone. But his parents said he should go, there was no future there. They said, *Look at all the people that went to America. Look at all the money they sent home. Look at all the things they brought back.* And he knew the decision wasn't really his to make. His father was too weak to work after his heart attack. His mother could only take on so many extra jobs. His brother and sister needed clothes, school supplies, food on the table.

"Where do you work?" Heaven asked, turning on her stool. Daniel thought that she was pretty. He'd come to like white girls because they didn't smell always of the fields or carry dirt and dust in their hair when they came to bed.

"Wherever I'm needed," he said.

Daniel had come young enough that he picked up the

language quickly, not like some of the older men who rode in the backs of trucks with him that would never be able to wipe the hard syllables from their mouths, their past always betraying them.

"Do you like it?"

"Sometimes, but it's not what I thought it would be." He thought of the fields, of the dirt, of all he hated about the routine of his days.

"How about you? Do you like this?"

"It's a job," Heaven said, and he knew exactly what she meant.

"And when you're not here?" he continued.

"I read a lot. I should get paid for that, don't you think? Ever hear of a book about those people who live their entire lives underground in the subways below New York City?"

"Subway people?" Daniel asked in mock surprise just to prod the conversation along.

"Yeah, actually. I carry it with me so I have something to read on the way home. Wait right here just a sec."

Heaven got off the bar stool and disappeared behind a wine-colored velvet curtain. Daniel swirled the lime in his beer.

When she returned she handed him a book with a black and white cover: *The Mole People: Life in the Tunnels Beneath New York City.*

"The cops won't even go after them anymore. They've stockpiled weapons."

Heaven's name came on between songs. She said she had to go. It was her turn. She left the book on the bar and Daniel continued to flip through it. There were more black and white pictures of a man and his dog, a couple, entire rooms decorated to resemble someone's version of civilization as much as possible. He read some of their stories. How some swore they would never go back up to the top. No matter what. Daniel didn't go to the stage and felt better that at least some other people had walked in to take his place. It was, after all, a slow night.

When Heaven returned, her breathing was a bit heavier, her skin coated with light sweat.

"Crazy, isn't it?" she asked.

Yes, it was crazy, Daniel thought. He also thought of what he would never ask: *If so many souls live in shadows below ground, how many more exist in shadows above ground? How many like him in other countries too small for anyone to care?*

Instead he said, "Wouldn't their skin turn pale from being in the dark all that time?" He thought of his own skin, a dark gold that got a bit darker at times, but never any lighter.

"I dunno. But I'm telling you. You don't want to be caught down there with these people. They're pissed off. Angry at what the world has done to them, as if everyone else is responsible for them choosing to live down there with the rats."

"Some never choose," Daniel said in a soft voice, looking

down at his hands. He closed the book and handed it to her.

"Do you want a dance?" Heaven asked after a long enough pause.

"What?"

"A dance. Do you want one?"

"No thanks. It's getting late."

It was a lie. It wasn't even midnight yet. But Daniel didn't want to admit that he didn't have enough money. Starting with his first day's pay, Daniel sent money back home. When he called for the first couple of years, his parents were thankful, happy to hear his voice. Then his father's health got worse. His sister needed an outfit. Could he send a bit more? He sent a bit more. Could he possibly send money for this or that, it'd be so nice if he could. Daniel could. He sent what he had. Kept enough to get by.

One day on the phone he said, "Mom, I think I'm going to come home." The long distance voice crackled on the other end, "Why would you do that? What's here Daniel? Nothing. There's nothing for you here. There you can work, make money."

Daniel understood. He'd been sent to America so he could have a future, possibilities, so those left behind at home could have the same. If he stayed out of trouble, out of sight, he could continue to work and send money through Western Union. He could eat their food, wear their clothes, learn their language and laugh at the same jokes. He could be in both worlds, body in one, memories in the other.

Heaven had gotten up from her stool and tried to find someone else to take her up on the offer of a dance. He knew she would take on a different persona with every person she met, would change to better fit the moment. He understood what needed to be done. Daniel watched her in her black heels, making her way among the tables and chairs and lights. When one man shook his head, she moved on. He wondered whom was she sending her money to? What was she working for? She'd said that everyone there came for a reason. What was her reason? What family, what hungry mouth was waiting at home expecting a meal on the table, never asking how or where it came from?

Daniel tipped his bottle back and swallowed warm beer. He decided he wouldn't go and wait on the same corner in the morning. There were always other corners. As he walked out of one darkness into the other dark of night, Daniel noticed the light of a lamppost casting a quivering glow down to the pavement. Hundreds of dizzy white flies beat themselves against the bulb. They looked like snowflakes picked up and carried by a gust of wind, floating for a while longer, delaying the inevitable.

Fomite
Burlington, Vermont

Fomite is a literary press whose authors and artists explore the human condition—political, cultural, personal and historical—in poetry and prose.

A fomite is a medium capable of transmitting infectious organisms from one individual to another.

"The activity of art is based on the capacity of people to be infected by the feelings of others." Tolstoy, *What Is Art?*

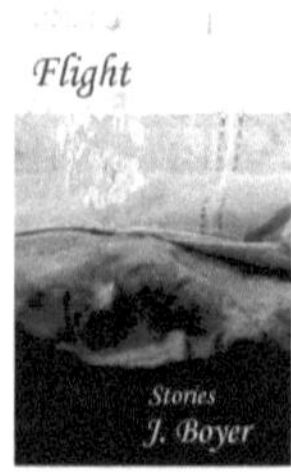

Flight and Other Stories - Jay Boyer

In *Flight and Other Stories,* we're with the fattest woman on earth as she draws her last breaths and her soul ascends toward its final reward. We meet a divorcee who can fly with no more effort than flapping her arms. We follow a middle-aged butler whose love affair with a young woman leads him first to the mysteries of bondage and then to the pleasures of malice. Story by story, we set foot into worlds so strange as to seem all but surreal, yet everything feels familiar, each moment rings true. And that's when we recognize we're in the hands of one of America's truly original talents.

Loisaida - Dan Chodorokoff

Catherine, a young anarchist estranged from her parents and squatting in an abandoned building on New York's Lower East Side, is fighting with her boyfriend and conflicted about her work on an underground newspaper. After learning of a developer's plans to demolish a community garden, Catherine builds an alliance with a group of Puerto Rican community activists. Together they confront the confluence of politics, money, and real estate that rule Manhattan. All the while she learns important lessons from her great-grandmother's life in the Yiddish anarchist movement that flourished on the Lower East Side at the turn of the century. In this coming-of-age story, family saga, and tale of urban politics, Dan Chodorkoff explores the "principle of hope" and examines how memory and imagination inform social change.

Improvisational Arguments - Anna Faktorovich

Improvisational Arguments is written in free verse to capture the essence of modern problems and triumphs. The poems clearly relate short, frequently humorous, and occasionally tragic stories about travels to exotic and unusual places, fantastic realms, abnormal jobs, artistic innovations, political objections, and misadventures with love.

Fomite
Burlington, Vermont

Loosestrife - Greg Delanty

This book is a chronicle of complicity in our modern lives, a witnessing of war and the destruction of our planet. It is also an attempt to adjust the more destructive blueprint myths of our society. Often our cultural memory tells us to keep quiet about the aspects that are most challenging to our ethics, to forget the violations we feel and tremors that keep us distant and numb.

Carts and Other Stories - Zdravka Evtimova

Roots and wings are the key words that best describe the short story collection *Carts and Other Stories,* by Zdravka Evtimova. The book is emotionally multilayered and memorable because of its internal power, vitality and ability to touch both your heart and your mind. Within its pages, the reader discovers new perspectives and true wealth, and learns to see the world with different eyes. The collection lives on the borders of different cultures. *Carts and Other Stories* will take the reader to wild and powerful Bulgarian mountains, to silver rains in Brussels, to German quiet winter streets, and to wind-bitten crags in Afghanistan. This book lives for those seeking to discover the beauty of the world around them, and will have them appreciating what they have—and perhaps what they have lost as well.

The Listener Aspires to the Condition of Music - Barry Goldensohn

"I know of no other selected poems that selects on one theme, but this one does, charting Goldensohn's career-long attraction to music's performance, consolations and its august, thrilling, scary and clownish charms. Does all art aspire to the condition of music as Pater claimed, exhaling in a swoon toward that one class act? Goldensohn is more aware than the late 19th century of the overtones of such breathing: his poems thoroughly round out those overtones in a poet's lifetime of listening."

John Peck, poet, editor, Fellow of the American Academy of Rome

The Co-Conspirator's Tale - Ron Jacobs

There's a place where love and mistrust are never at peace; where duplicity and deceit are the universal currency. *The Co-Conspirator's Tale* takes place within this nebulous firmament. There are crimes committed by the police in the name of the law. Excess in the name of revolution. The combination leaves death in its wake and the survivors struggling to find justice in a San Francisco Bay Area noir by the author of the underground classic *The Way the Wind Blew: A History of the Weather Underground* and the novel *Short Order Frame Up.*

Fomite
Burlington, Vermont

Short Order Frame Up - Ron Jacobs

1975. America has lost its war in Vietnam and Cambodia. Racially tinged riots are tearing the city of Boston apart. The politics and counterculture of the 1960s are disintegrating into nothing more than sex, drugs, and rock and roll. The Boston Red Sox are on one of their improbable runs toward a postseason appearance. In a suburban town in Maryland, a young couple are murdered and another young man is accused. The couple are white and the accused is black. It is up to his friends and family to prove he is innocent. This is a story of suburban ennui, race, murder, and injustice. Religion and politics, liberal lawyers and racist cops. In *Short Order Frame Up*, Ron Jacobs has written a piece of crime fiction that exposes the wound that is US racism. Two cultures existing side by side and across generations—a river very few dare to cross. His characters work and live with and next to each other, often unaware of each other's real life. When the murder occurs, however, those people that care about the man charged must cross that river and meet somewhere in between in order to free him from (what is to them) an obvious miscarriage of justice.

All the Sinners Saints - Ron Jacobs

A young draftee named Victor Willard goes AWOL in Germany after an altercation with a commanding officer. Porgy is an African-American GI involved with the international Black Panthers and German radicals. Victor and a female radical named Ana fall in love. They move into Ana's room in a squatted building near the US base in Frankfurt. The international campaign to free Black revolutionary Angela Davis is coming to Frankfurt. Porgy and Ana are key organizers and Victor spends his days and nights selling and smoking hashish, while becoming addicted to heroin. Police and narcotics agents are keeping tabs on them all. Politics, love, and drugs. Truths, lies, and rock and roll. *All the Sinners Saints* is a story of people seeking redemption in a world awash in sin.

Roadworthy Creature, Roadworthy Craft - Kate Magill

Words fail but the voice struggles on. The culmination of a decade's worth of performance poetry, *Roadworthy Creature, Roadworthy Craft* is Kate Magill's first full-length publication. In lines that are sinewy yet delicate, Magill's poems explore the terrain where idea and action meet, where bodies and words commingle to form a strange new flesh, a breathing text, an "I" that spirals outward from itself.

Fomite
Burlington, Vermont

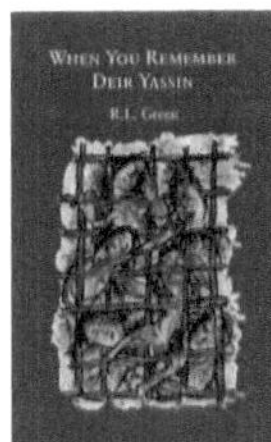

When You Remember Deir Yassin - R. L. Green

When You Remember Deir Yassin is a collection of poems by R. L. Green, an American Jewish writer, on the subject of the occupation and destruction of Palestine. Green comments: "Outspoken Jewish critics of Israeli crimes against humanity have, strangely, been called 'anti-Semitic' as well as 'self-hating Jews.' As a Jewish critic of the Israeli government, I have come to accept these accusations as a stamp of approval and a badge of honor, signifying my own fealty to a central element of Jewish identity and ethics: one must be a lover of truth and a friend to the oppressed, and stand with the victims of tyranny, not with the tyrants, despite tribal loyalty or self-advancement. These poems were written as expressions of outrage, and of grief, and to encourage my sisters and brothers of every cultural or national grouping to speak out against injustice, to try to save Palestine, and in so doing, to reclaim for myself my own place as part of the Jewish people."

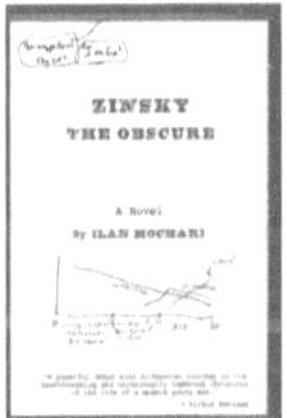

Zinsky the Obscure - Ilan Mochari

"If your childhood is brutal, your adulthood becomes a daily attempt to recover: a quest for ecstasy and stability in recompense for their early absence." So states the 30-year-old Ariel Zinsky, whose bachelor-like lifestyle belies the torturous youth he is still coming to grips with. As a boy, he struggles with the beatings themselves; as a grownup, he struggles with the world's indifference to them. *Zinsky the Obscure* is his life story, a humorous chronicle of his search for a redemptive ecstasy through sex, an entrepreneurial sports obsession, and finally, the cathartic exercise of writing it all down. Fervently recounting both the comic delights and the frightening horrors of a life in which he feels—always—that he is not like all the rest, Zinsky survives the worst and relishes the best with idiosyncratic style, as his heartbreak turns into self-awareness and his suicidal ideation into self-regard. A vivid evocation of the all-consuming nature of lust and ambition—and the forces that drive them.

The Derivation of Cowboys & Indians - Joseph D. Reich

The Derivation of Cowboys & Indians represents a profound journey, a breakdown of the American Dream from a social, cultural, historical, and spiritual point of view. Reich examines in concise detail the loss of the collective unconscious, commenting on our contemporary postmodern culture with its self-interested excesses, on where and how things all go wrong, and how social/political practice rarely meets its original proclamations and promises. Reich's surreal and self-effacing satire brings this troubling message home. *The Derivation of Cowboys & Indians* is a desperate search and struggle for America's literal, symbolic, and spiritual home.

Fomite
Burlington, Vermont

Kasper Planet: Comix and Tragix - Peter Schumann

The British call him Punch; the Italians, Pulchinella; the Russians, Petruchka; the Native Americans, Coyote. These are the figures we may know. But every culture that worships authority will breed a Punch-like, anti-authoritarian resister. Yin and yang—it has to happen. The Germans call him Kasper. Truth-telling and serious pranking are dangerous professions when going up against power. Bradley Manning sits naked in solitary; Julian Assange is pursued by Interpol, Obama's Department of Justice, and Amazon.com. But—in contrast to merely human faces— masks and theater can often slip through the bars. Consider our American Kaspers: Charlie Chaplin, Woody Guthrie, Abby Hoffman, the Yes Men—theater people all, utilizing various forms to seed critique. Their profiles and tactics have evolved along with those of their enemies. Who are the bad guys that call forth the Kaspers? Over the last half century, with his Bread & Puppet Theater, Peter Schumann has been tireless in naming them, excoriating them with Kasperdom....
from Marc Estrin's Foreword to Planet Kasper

Views Cost Extra - L.E. Smith

Views that inspire, that calm, or that terrify—all come at some cost to the viewer. In *Views Cost Extra* you will find a New Jersey high school preppy who wants to inhabit the "perfect" cowboy movie, a rural mailman disgusted with the residents of his town who wants to live with the penguins, an ailing screen-writer who strikes a deal with Johnny Cash to reverse an old man's failures, an old man who ponders a young man's suicide attempt, a one-armed blind blues singer who wants to reunite with the car that took her arm on the assembly line— and more. These stories suggest that we must pay something to live even ordinary lives.

The Empty Notebook Interrogates Itself - Susan Thomas

The Empty Notebook began its life as a very literal metaphor for a few weeks of what the poet thought was writer's block, but was really the struggle of an eccentric persona to take over her working life. It won. And for the next three years everything she wrote came to her in the voice of the Empty Notebook, who, as the notebook began to fill itself, became rather opinionated, changed gender, alternately acted as bully and victim, had many bizarre adventures in exotic locales, and developed a somewhat politically incorrect attitude. It then began to steal the voices and forms of other poets and tried to immortalize itself in various poetry reviews. It is now thrilled to collect itself in one slim volume.

Fomite

Burlington, Vermont

My God, What Have We Done? - Susan Weiss

In a world afflicted with war, toxicity, and hunger, does what we do in our private lives really matter? Fifty years after the creation of the atomic bomb at Los Alamos, newlyweds Pauline and Clifford visit that once-secret city on their honeymoon, compelled by Pauline's fascination with Oppenheimer, the soulful scientist. The two stories emerging from this visit reverberate back and forth between the loneliness of a new mother at home in Boston and the isolation of an entire community dedicated to the development of the bomb. While Pauline struggles with unforeseen challenges of family life, Oppenheimer and his crew reckon with forces beyond all imagining.

Finally the years of frantic research on the bomb culminate in a stunning test explosion that echoes a rupture in the couple's marriage. Against the backdrop of a civilization that's out of control, Pauline begins to understand the complex, potentially explosive physics of personal relationships.

At once funny and dead serious, *My God, What Have We Done?* sifts through the ruins left by the bomb in search of a more worthy human achievement.

As It Is On Earth - Peter M. Wheelwright

Four centuries after the Reformation Pilgrims sailed up the down-flowing watersheds of New England, Taylor Thatcher, irreverent scion of a fallen family of Maine Puritans, is still caught in the turbulence.

In his errant attempts to escape from history, the young college professor is further unsettled by his growing attraction to Israeli student Miryam Bluehm as he is swept by Time through the "family thing"—from the tangled genetic and religious history of his New England parents to the redemptive birthday secret of Esther Fleur Noire Bishop, the Cajun-Passamaquoddy woman who raised him and his younger half-cousin/half-brother, Bingham.

The landscapes, rivers, and tidal estuaries of Old New England and the Mayan Yucatan are also casualties of history in Thatcher's story of Deep Time and re-discovery of family on Columbus Day at a high-stakes gambling casino, rising in resurrection over the starlit bones of a once-vanquished Pequot Indian tribe.

Suite for Three Voices - Derek Furr

Suite for Three Voices is a dance of prose genres, teeming with intense human life in all its humor and sorrow. A son uncovers the horrors of his father's wartime experience, a hitchhiker in a muumuu guards a mysterious parcel, a young man foresees his brother's brush with death on September 11. A Victorian poetess encounters space aliens and digital archives, a runner hears the voice of a dead friend in the song of an indigo bunting, a teacher seeks wisdom from his students' errors and Neil Young.

By frozen waterfalls and neglected graveyards, along highways at noon and rivers at dusk, in the sound of bluegrass, Beethoven, and Emily Dickinson, the essays and fiction in this collection offer moments of vision.

Fomite
Burlington, Vermont

Travers' Inferno - *L.E. Smith*

In the 1970's, churches began to burn in Burlington, Vermont. If it was arson, no one or no reason could be found to blame. This book suggests arson, but makes no claim to historical realism. It claims, instead, to capture the dizzying 70's zeitgeist of aggressive utopian movements, distrust in authority, escapist alternative lifestyles, and a bewildered society of onlookers. In the tradition of John Gardner's *Sunlight Dialogues*, the characters of *Travers' Inferno* are colorful and damaged, sometimes comical, sometimes tragic, looking for meaning through desperate acts. Travers Jones, the protagonist, is grounded in the transcendent—philosophy, epilepsy, arson as purification—and mystified by the opposite sex, haunted by an absent father and directed by an uncle with a grudge. He is seduced by a professor's wife and chased by an endearing if ineffective sergeant of police. There are secessionist Quebecois involved in these church burns who are murdering as well as pilfering and burning. There are changing alliances, violent deaths, lovemaking, and a belligerent cat.

Still Time - Michael Cocchiarale

Still Time is a collection of twenty-five short and shorter stories exploring tensions that arise in a variety of contemporary relationships: a young boy must deal with the wrath of his out-of-work father; a woman runs into a man twenty years after an awkward sexual encounter; a wife, unable to conceive, imagines her own murder, as well as the reaction of her emotionally distant husband; a soon-to-be-tenured English professor tries to come to terms with her husband's shocking return to the religion of his youth; an assembly line worker, married for thirty years, discovers the surprising secret life of his recently hospitalized wife. Whether a few hundred or a few thousand words, these and other stories in the collection depict characters at moments of deep crisis. Some feel powerless, overwhelmed—unable to do much to change the course of their lives. Others rise to the occasion and, for better or for worse, say or do the thing that might transform them for good. Even in stories with the most troubling of endings, there remains the possibility of redemption. For each of the characters, there is still time.

Raven or Crow - Joshua Amses

Marlowe has recently moved back home to Vermont after flunking his first term at a private college in the Midwest, when his sort-of girlfriend, Eleanor, goes missing. The circumstances surrounding Eleanor's disappearance stand to reveal more about Marlowe than he is willing to allow. Rather than report her missing, he resolves to find Eleanor himself. *Raven or Crow* is the story of mistakes rooted in the ambivalence of being young and without direction.

Fomite

Burlington, Vermont

Signed Confessions - *Tom Walker*

Guilt and a desperate need to repent drive the antiheroes in Tom Walker's dark (and often darkly funny) stories:

-A gullible journalist falls for the 40-year-old stripper he profiles in a magazine.

-A faithless husband abandons his family and joins a support group for lost souls.

-A merciless prosecuting attorney grapples with the suicide of his gay son.

-An aging misanthrope must make amends to five former victims.

-An egoistic naval hero is haunted by apparitions of his dead wife and a mysterious little girl.

The seven tales in *Signed Confessions* measure how far guilty men will go to obtain a forgiveness no one can grant but themselves.

The Housing Market - *Joseph D. Reich*

In Joseph Reich's most recent social and cultural, contemporary satireof suburbia entitled, "The Housing market: a comfortable place to jumpoff the end of the world," the author addresses the absurd, postmodern elements of what it means, or for that matter not, to try & cope & function, and survive and thrive, or live and die in the repetitive and existential, futile and self-destructive, homogenized, monochromatic landscape of a brutal and bland, collective unconscious, which can

spiritually result in a gradual wasting away and erosion of the senses
or conflict and crisis of a desperate, disproportionate 'situational
depression,' triggering and leading the narrator to feel constantly
abandoned and stranded, more concretely or proverbially spoken,
"the eternal stranger," where when caught between the fight or
flight psychological phenomena, naturally repels him and causes
him to flee and return without him even knowing it into the wild,
while by sudden circumstance and coincidence discovers it
surrounds the illusory-like circumference of these selfsame
Monopoly board cul-de-sacs and dead ends. Most specifically,
what can happen to a solitary, thoughtful, and independent
thinker when being stagnated in the triangulation of a cookie-
cutter, oppressive culture of a homeowner's association; a
memoir all written in critical and didactic, poetic stanzas
and passages, and out of desperation, when freedom and
control get taken, what he is forced to do in the illusion
of 'free will and volition,' something like the derivative
art of a smart and ironic and social and cultural satire.

Fomite
Burlington, Vermont

Love's Labours - Jack Pulaski

In the four stories and two novellas that comprise *Love's Labors* the protagonists, Ben and Laura, discover in their fervid romance and long marriage their interlocking fates, and the histories that preceded their births. They also learned something of the paradox between love and all the things it brings to its beneficiaries: bliss, disaster, duty, tragedy, comedy, the grotesque, and tenderness.

Ben and Laura's story is also the particularly American tale of immigration to a new world. Laura's story begins in Puerto Rico, and Ben's lineage is Russian-Jewish. They meet in City College of New York, a place at least analogous to a melting pot. Laura struggles to rescue her brother from gang life and heroin. She is mother to her younger sister; their mother Consuelo is the financial mainstay of the family and consumed by work. Despite filial obligations, Laura aspires to be a serious painter. Ben writes, cares for, and is caught up in the misadventures and surreal stories of his younger schizophrenic brother. Laura is also a story teller as powerful and enchanting as Scheherazade. Ben struggles to survive such riches, and he and Laura endure.

Meanwell - *Janice Miller Potter*

Meanwell is a twenty-four-poem sequence in which a female servant searches for identity and meaning in the shadow of her mistress, poet Anne Bradstreet. Although Meanwell herself is a fiction, someone like her could easily have existed among Bradstreet's known but unnamed domestic servants. Through Meanwell's eyes, Bradstreet emerges as a human figure during the Great Migration of the 1600s, a period in which the Massachusetts Bay Colony was fraught with physical and political dangers. Through Meanwell, the feelings of women, silenced during the midwife Anne Hutchinson's fiery trial before the Puritan ministers, are finally acknowledged. In effect, the poems are about the making of an American rebel. Through her conflicted conscience, we witness Meanwell's transformation from a powerless English waif to a mythic American who ultimately chooses wilderness over the civilization she has experienced.

Entanglements - Tony Magistrale

A poet and a painter may employ different mediums to express the same snow-blown afternoon in January, but sometimes they find a way to capture the moment in such a way that their respective visions still manage to stir a reverberation, a connection. In part, that's what *Entanglements* seeks to do. Not so much for the poems and paintings to speak directly to one another, but for them to stir points of similarity.

Fomite
Burlington, Vermont

Four-Way Stop - Sherry Olson

If *Thank You* were the only prayer, as Meister Eckhart has suggested, it would be enough, and Sherry Olson's poetry, in her second book, *Four-Way Stop*, would be one. Radical attention, deep love, and dedication to kindness illuminate these poems and the stories she tells us, which are drawn from her own life: with family, with friends, and wherever she travels, with strangers – who to Olson, never are strangers, but kin.

Even at the difficult intersections, as in the title poem, *Four-Way Stop,* Olson experiences – and offers – hope, showing us how, *completely unsupervised,* people take turns, with *kindness waving each other on.* Olson writes, knowing that (to quote Czeslaw Milosz) *What surrounds us, here and now, is not guaranteed.* To this world, with her poems, Olson brings – and teaches – attention, generosity, compassion, and appreciative joy.
—Carol Henrikson

Visiting Hours - *Jennifer Anne Moses*

Visiting Hours, a novel-in-stories, explores the lives of people not normally met on the page—-AIDS patients and those who care for them. Set in Baton Rouge, Louisiana, and written with large and frequent dollops of humor, the book is a profound meditation on faith and love in the face of illness and poverty.

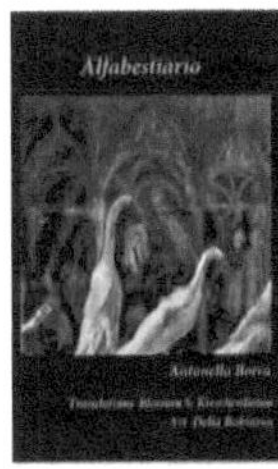

Alfabestiario
AlphaBetaBestiario - *Antonello Borra*
Animals have always understood that mankind is not fully at home in the world. Bestiaries, hoping to teach, send out warnings. This one, of course, aims at doing the same.

Writing a review on Amazon, Good Reads, Shelfari, Library Thing or other social media sites for readers will help the progress of independent publishing. To submit a review, go to the book page on any of the sites and follow the links for reviews. Books from independent presses rely on reader to reader communications.